C000150303

Caroline Saves the Blacksmith Print Edition
Copyright © 2023 by Nina Jarrett. All rights reserved.
Published by Rogue Press.
Edited by Katie Jackson

For more information, contact author Nina Jarrett. www.ninajarrett.com

CAROLINE SAVES THE BLACKSMITH

INCONVENIENT BRIDES
BOOK FIVE

NINA JARRETT

ROGUE
PRESS

Thank you to the tradespeople of Colonial Williamsburg for bringing history to life and answering my questions about trades in the 1700s with patience and expertise.

And, on the topic of history, I would like to thank my wonderful editor, Katie Jackson, whose sharp eyes are always on the lookout for anachronisms. She has not only helped me craft better stories, but helped me to ensure that they were as true to the era as possible.

PROLOGUE: THE BEGINNING

EARLY AUTUMN, 1818

*T*ears streamed down Caroline Brown's cheeks as she packed her valise and a small trunk provided by Mrs. Harris.

She was leaving Baydon Hall, the only true home she had ever known, for a new position in the local doctor's household that Mrs. Harris had arranged for her. Yet she did not deserve the post.

I deserve to be thrown out of the manor, without any assistance, for what I have done.

Regret and shame warred in her chest, and her body felt too small and tight to contain all the emotions threatening to brim over.

It is all my fault.

She had lost her home, her friends, and her self-respect, and for what? For a few moments of pleasure here or there in a libertine's arms. So desperate for attention from a man, she had succumbed to temptation these past weeks and betrayed a dear friend.

Three days earlier, Miss Annabel Ridley, the daughter of the baron at Baydon Hall, had caught her dallying with the lady's betrothed, the Earl of Saunton, in the stables. Lord Saunton had failed to defend her, and Miss Annabel had been rightfully enraged, unwilling to see or speak to Caroline. Nevertheless, Miss Annabel had seen fit to provide her a reference for her position as a maid and bade Mrs. Harris, the housekeeper, to find her employment elsewhere.

It was incredibly generous given the circumstances, but Miss Annabel had always been kind. As a girl, Miss Annabel had taught Caroline to read and bestowed gifts of fabrics, ribbons, and threads on her birthday each year to encourage her interest in sewing. Now, despite the horrendous betrayal, Miss Annabel had assisted Caroline with her future position.

But the young mistress of Baydon Hall was furious and distraught. She had instructed that Caroline remain out of sight in the kitchens and leave the Hall as quickly as possible.

Miss Annabel's unexpected generosity added to Caroline's crushing guilt. She wished she could plead for forgiveness, to assure Miss Annabel that she had seen the error of her ways and wanted to make amends for their relationship that had been so influential in her life.

But she had no amends to offer.

I am a fallen woman.

Worse, she was a disloyal friend, undeserving of the help she was receiving.

Her grandmother would turn in her grave to hear how Caroline had thrown away the opportunity afforded her by the old woman's friendship with Mrs. Harris. One of her last acts before dying had been to write to the housekeeper to request her assistance with the then-thirteen-year-old Caroline, who was about to lose her last living relation. Mrs.

Harris had offered employment as a favor to her old friend, and Caroline had been summoned into service at Baydon Hall.

Since Grandmama had died, the servants, along with Miss Annabel, were Caroline's only family. She had betrayed all of them, ruining Miss Annabel's happiness in the process.

A few tender words from a handsome nobleman, and compliments to her figure, and Caroline had allowed herself to be lured into carnal relations with a rogue. Fresh sobs tore through her chest, despair a physical pain. How would she ever forgive herself for what she had done?

CHAPTER ONE: THE MEETING

8 NOVEMBER 1820

*C*aroline waved goodbye to Mr. and Mrs. Thompson and their daughter and gently shut the door of her shop, Mrs. Brown's Elegant Millinery and Dress-Rooms, to draw an exhilarated breath. The odor of wood, fabric, and beeswax invaded her senses, and she gave a deep sigh of happiness.

The shop was now hers and hers alone. As of today, she was officially a modiste. The proprietress of her own business. Well … hers except for the interest-free loan from Lord Saunton that she must pay off as profits allowed.

Caroline still experienced moments of unreality, thinking she had dreamed all that had happened in the past few months. Lord Saunton had summoned her to London, nearly two years after the incident in the stables, to apologize for his disruption of her life. He had offered her financial assistance, but instead of accepting his charity, Caroline had seized the opportunity to demand the loan that Miss Annabel had intended to provide after her planned marriage to Lord Saunton.

Of course, Miss Annabel never married Lord Saunton. Caroline had learned from the local gossip in Filminster that Miss Annabel had married the Duke of Halmesbury and now lived somewhere nearby in Wiltshire.

Lord Saunton had corrected his wayward behavior to marry a young woman in London, for which Caroline could only be grateful now that he had assisted her with her dreams to open her own dress-rooms in his effort to make amends. He had set his man, Mr. Johnson, to find a suitable location for her shop and advise her on how to make her business venture a success.

The lurid path to her proprietorship must remain a secret now that she had a fresh start in Wiltshire. It would ruin her business before it had begun if the local townspeople learned she was a fallen woman—or if they assumed she was currently a kept woman.

That will not happen.

Those who knew the truth of her past were the Duke and Duchess of Halmesbury, the Baron of Filminster, Mrs. Harris, Lord and Lady Saunton, along with his men Johnson and Long, and Caroline herself. Thus far, all the parties involved appeared to have practiced discretion, and Caroline was the only one living in Chatternwell. She supposed Mr. Thompson, the earl's half-brother, might be aware of her situation, but he had not intimated such during his visit.

As long as Caroline focused on her business, and did not form any personal relationships, she could keep her secret. As she had done in Filminster when she had worked for the local doctor.

For months after being caught in the stables, Caroline had lived in the shadow of fear that her secret would come out. But then her book learning and knowledge of numbers, taught to her by Miss Annabel to prepare her for running a business one day, had resulted in a promotion to housekeeper of the doctor's household.

That had been the day that Caroline had finally realized her secret was safe, and that no one intended to reveal her shameful behavior. She had vowed to keep her mind on work, and to avoid private connections, and thus she had thrived as the doctor's housekeeper. If she maintained that stratagem here in Wiltshire, she would succeed here in her new home, too.

Caroline had been in Chatternwell for two months, preparing for today's shop opening, and she was satisfied with the progress she had made.

Lord Saunton and his brother, Mr. Barclay Thompson, a renowned architect, had made a point of endorsing her work to the local townspeople on her opening day. Lord Saunton had ordered a banyan for himself, rather loudly for the other patrons to overhear, and Mr. Thompson's wife and daughter each had orders for carriage dresses.

Word that an earl was in the modiste's shop had quickly spread. Caroline had gained valuable introductions to other merchants, as well as several orders for expensive gowns, when the local well-to-do had hurried in to see the earl and his family and to meet the unknown modiste who boasted the custom of such lauded nobility.

When Lord Saunton had first informed her that he intended to attend her opening day, Caroline had been concerned about her reputation. Surely, the townsfolk would suspect what their connection must be? But the earl had taken pains to attend along with family members, so no hint of impropriety would taint her special day. Loud remarks to his brother and sister-in-law regarding their mutual visit to his unoccupied nearby estate, Chatternwell

House, and his surprise to discover such an elegant and fashionable shop in town, had been carefully stated within earshot of ladies perusing expensive fabrics. Caroline appreciated the subtlety he had employed despite the oddity of their past that caused their exchanges to be stilted with caution.

She still experienced flashes of disbelief that she was truly here, running her own shop. Looking about at the display of gloves and scarves by the window, the bolts of richly-colored fabrics fitted into neat cubbyholes that soared up the wall to the very ceilings, she hummed to herself with happiness.

Running her hand along a walnut counter, Caroline admitted she would never have dared to dream of such a day after what she had done to Miss Annabel. The goal of her own shop had seemed ridiculous, but when the unsought opportunity had presented itself, she had grabbed it with both hands, recognizing it as her last chance to pursue the future she had imagined and then lost. Now that it was realized, she would do nothing to endanger her new life.

Here in the town of Chatternwell, she was a respected member of the community and the corruption of her past was a distant memory. A memory she would hold close as a warning that she must never again form any serious attachments lest she destroy them. Work, work, work was the answer to the question of her happiness. It was her penance for her past mistakes.

Caroline smiled when she caught sight of a little girl outside who was pressing her face to the window. The girl often came by and stared at the ribbon display, but had so far not had the courage to step inside. The little mite sorely needed a ribbon to tie back her muss of mousy brown hair, and it tempted Caroline to invite her in.

Tidying the fashion plates on the counter, she hummed quietly. Glancing back at the window where sunlight illuminated the small figure, Caroline frowned when she noticed something she had not expected.

Usually the girl was fascinated, gaping at the colorful ribbons as if the treasures of the world were before her. Today her shoulders were slumped down, and Caroline thought she saw tears dripping down the girl's cheeks. She straightened in alarm, uncertain what to do.

She did not know the girl or her parents, but someone loved the child. Although her clothes were worn, they were clean and mended. Biting her lip, and reminding herself she was to maintain a friendly rapport with the townsfolk while avoiding close ties, Caroline walked around the counter to the front. Hesitating for just a second, she drew a deep breath and opened the door.

* * *

WILLIAM JACKSON STOOD at the mullioned window of the Chatternwell post office, waiting for the clerk to finish with Mrs. Butterworth. With a bored sigh, he watched little Annie Greer peering into the window of the new dress-rooms across the road.

He wondered how the Greers were doing. He really should have called on them more often than he had done. Brian Greer had been in the same regiment, and William had not known him very well, but the man had lost his life the same day as William's cousin, Charles, at the farmhouse they had defended against Boney's army.

William's only excuse was that after decades of war with the French, every town in England was littered with widows, so Annie and Mrs. Greer had simply slipped his mind.

A slight frown of concern settled between his brows when he noticed that Annie's shoulders were quivering something fierce. Was the little girl sobbing?

Stepping forward to take a closer look, he noticed the shop door open and a woman step out. His breath caught as she came into view, Annie Greer's plight temporarily forgotten. This must be the recently arrived mantua-maker, according to the town gossips, but no one had mentioned how young or lovely the proprietress was.

Her wheat-colored hair was swept back in an elegant coif to reveal a fair, oval face. She had a pointed chin, and a thick sweep of lashes framed eyes he could not discern the color of. A wide, full mouth was at once soft and determined, and the mulberry gown she wore offset her coloring in the most attractive way.

It had been many years since William had felt any emotion. He had ruthlessly killed any feelings after that day of war at Waterloo, when his uncontrolled battle rage had overtaken his senses.

He had welcomed the numbness when he had awoken in the field hospital after his injuries, not wishing to feel the agony of seeing his dear cousin cut down in battle. He had especially welcomed it when he had returned to Chatternwell five years ago to inform his uncle and aunt of the death of their beloved son, news of which had broken their very souls right in front of him.

William had vowed to himself to maintain this state of logic, immune to the pain of the past, as he had stepped out of his role of nephew to the blacksmith and his wife, and stepped into the role of de facto son as his penance for having convinced Charles to fight Boney's army by his side.

But that was the past which he had closed the door on long ago.

In the present, he watched with curiosity as the young woman beckoned Annie Greer into her shop. For the first time in years, he felt a shiver of unexpected anticipation slowly traverse from his chest, up his throat to well in his mouth, as if his heart had woken up and taken a solitary beat.

As the two females disappeared into the interior of the shop, William acknowledged the truth of it. He needed to stay away from Mrs. Brown's Elegant Millinery and Dress-Rooms if he was to maintain his peace of mind.

* * *

CAROLINE USHERED the weeping girl to the back room. As they walked through the doorway, Caroline swept the curtain open so she might see the front of the shop.

Mrs. Jones looked up from the worktable where she and her eldest daughter, Mary Beth, were sewing gowns. The seamstress's rounded face creased into a wide smile. "Mrs. Brown, there is fresh tea in the pot."

The seamstress beckoned to near the fireplace with the needle held in her hand. Mrs. Jones and Mary Beth were positioned near the window where the best light was to be found.

Light was a seamstress's best friend. Caroline had lured the town's most talented to her shop with good pay and regular hours, and many of her employees worked from their homes. But Mrs. Jones and Mary Beth preferred to work in the back of the shop. They told her the light was better, but Caroline thought it might have to do with escaping their extensive family for some quiet and a spot of tea.

She nodded, placing the little girl at a workbench near the door, and headed to the teapot. Her grandmother had always said that there was no situation that a cup of tea could not improve. Whatever had caused the girl's distress was best disclosed with some fortitude.

The two women cast curious glances at the sniffling child before hesitantly bowing their heads back to their sewing,

Mary Beth continuing a tale about a fight that had broken out between the men at one of the taverns the night before.

Caroline poured out two cups of tea, adding a dash of milk to her own, but no sugar. She needed energy to work long hours as a shop owner, and she found that sugar caused fatigue, which she had no time for.

To the second cup, she added a lot of milk and extra sugar. If the child was anything like Caroline had been at her age, she would likely prefer it watered-down and sweet. And sugar was good for shock, according to the doctor Caroline had worked for, so perhaps the girl would need it.

Carrying the cups back to where the girl sat, Caroline placed them on the table before taking a seat across from her.

"What is your name, little one?"

"Annie," she responded hoarsely. "Annie Greer."

The child's tears had stopped, but her expression was desolate and her reddened eyes fixed on the cup in front of her. It gnawed at Caroline's gut to see the girl so distraught.

No personal relationships, do you hear?

Caroline squashed the inner voice. This was not the time nor place.

"And why are you so upset, Annie Greer?"

The girl was too lean. She was pale, with the dark hollows of someone undernourished. Caroline suspected the child might not have enough to eat, with her thin limbs and a dress that had been let out and mended many times.

"My mum is sending me away to Bath and I don't want to go!"

Caroline reached forward and tapped the teacup, encouraging the girl to drink. Annie lifted it to her lips and took a sip. She brightened slightly, and she sipped down the tea with gusto. When she set the cup down, only half of the milky tea remained and she appeared less stricken.

"What is in Bath?"

"My mum found someone who would take me on, but I can't leave her alone. Mum is sick, and she needs my help, so I must stay here with her."

"There is no one else to take care of her?"

"No. Just Mum and me. She tried to find a place for me here in Chatternwell, but no one needs me."

Caroline mused over this, sipping her tea. She did not have any apprentices yet because she was still living in rented rooms nearby and had not arranged a home for herself. No home meant no place to provide room and board to apprentices.

And you are to avoid entanglements with the townspeople!

"What kind of place in Bath?"

The little girl made a strangled sound. "Washerwoman."

Caroline winced. It was not a promising path for a lively young girl. There were far better ways to make a living. And safer places to live than a large town like Bath. Ways and places that had a future, but clearly Mrs. Greer was desperate.

Don't do it, Caroline! You swore not to get involved with other people!

Caroline recognized the truth of the warning, but once upon a time, she had been alone with her grandmother. When the old woman had ailed, it was a frightening time in her young life. Fortunately, Mrs. Harris had responded to Grandmama's request for help, promising to hire Caroline when the time came. Grandmama and Mrs. Harris had been colleagues at a dress shop before Mrs. Harris had been widowed.

Once Caroline started at Baydon Hall, Miss Annabel had learned of her interest in sewing and bade Mrs. Harris to apprentice her in the arts of millinery and mantua-making. Without that assistance, someone taking a chance on her,

Caroline would not have had the skills she needed to open her shop.

"Would you like to learn to sew?"

Annie looked up from her tea. Her tears were drying, but there remained little streaks down her cheeks. Caroline pulled out a handkerchief and leaned over to dab the girl's face.

"I can sew." Annie picked at the bodice of her dress to display a neat little darn near the sleeve.

"That is excellent work."

"Thank you."

Caroline breathed in deeply, realizing she was about to break her vow to herself. She had the means to help the little girl and her mum. And what was the point of being a business owner, a merchant, if she could not provide gainful employment to someone in need of help?

"How about I hire you as an apprentice?"

Annie lit up, then slumped. "I can't. I must go home at night to look after Mum. And we don't have any money now that she can't work so much. I have to find something that pays."

"I think we can arrange something. I do not have room and board to provide yet, so I would pay you the equivalent of what that would cost me. You can go home at night to look after your mum."

Annie beamed. "Truly? I can work in your shop and stay at home with Mum?"

There could be consequences to what she was contemplating. If Mrs. Greer failed to recover from her ill health, Caroline might find herself, for all intents and purposes, with a young daughter on her hands.

Are you really going to take this risk? This could get complicated!

Caroline made a decision. She would make an exception,

just this once. Because the girl needed a helping hand, just as Caroline had around her age, which she guessed to be about thirteen or so. "You can begin tomorrow if your mum agrees. Tell her to come see me in the morning, and if we reach an agreement, I will have a contract drawn up for her to sign."

Annie clapped her hands together, her expression joyful.

Caroline smiled back, before gesturing at the cup. "Finish your tea, Annie."

The girl did so in good spirits. When they were done, Caroline shooed her back to the front of the shop, where she accompanied her to the window display.

"As a seamstress and a member of my staff, it is important that you tie your hair back so you might see your work. Which ribbon would you like?"

Annie's little jaw dropped open as she turned to stare at the spools. "A ribbon? Of my own?"

"Pick one."

The child inspected the ribbons carefully, finally picking up a scarlet length with her diminutive forefingers. "Can I have this one?"

"You can." Caroline reached into a drawer under the counter to pull out her scissors, carefully measuring out and cutting a length of ribbon. Laying the ribbon down on the counter, she took hold of the girl's hair and combed it through with her fingers. Then she plaited it and tied it off with the ribbon, revealing the shells of Annie's little ears before draping the plait over the girl's shoulder so that Annie could see the bow.

"Cor! It is beautiful!"

Caroline smiled. "You will learn how to make many beautiful things here."

Annie left soon after, once they had agreed on a time for Mrs. Greer's visit. Despite her misgivings about forming close connections, Caroline felt she had made the correct decision.

* * *

WILLIAM HAD PURCHASED provisions and was returning to his cottage with his parcels under his arm, enjoying a rare respite from his work.

It should have taken only a few minutes to walk back, but somehow he had found himself hovering at the door of the mantua-maker. It was devilishly tempting to enter the shop under some pretext so he might see her in person. Perhaps confirm the color of her irises, and trace the shape of her sweet mouth with his eyes.

Or fingertips.

William stifled the urging of his inquisitive body as Annie Greer exited the dress-rooms, a huge smile making him think he must have misread her mood earlier when he had seen her from the window of the post office. She looked quite smart, with a neat but uncharacteristic plait and a red ribbon tying her hair.

"Enjoying your day, Annie?"

She beamed, nodding her head vigorously. "It is a wonderful day, Mr. Jackson. I am to be a seamstress!" she proclaimed loudly, before skipping away down the street in a flutter of skirts.

William shook his head in surprise. Had the young woman hired little Annie? He supposed it would be good news for Mrs. Greer. He had just been informed while about town that Mrs. Greer was suffering from ill health, and he had wondered if that was the cause of the scene he had witnessed earlier.

Everywhere he had gone today, women were talking about the new dressmaker and her delightful shop. It was commendable if Mrs. Brown had offered the young girl employment—something he might have done himself if he had been aware of the Greers' unfortunate circumstances.

He really should have returned home, especially now that he had confirmed that Annie was all right, but he found himself reluctant to walk off.

You should return home, William!

Something about the shop owner was calling him to visit her shop. But he had vowed to keep his distance from others. After losing Charles, and after the torrent of unruly emotions that had followed, William had known that work was the answer to his sanity. No emotions, just work.

Yet … he still hovered at the shop door.

This is ridiculous, William. Just go home!

He squared his shoulders and stepped in the direction of home.

* * *

IT WAS LATE AFTERNOON, almost closing time, when the shop door opened and closed. Caroline was mid counting spools of thread and scratched a number down on the notebook before swiveling, with a wide smile of greeting, to attend to the customer who had entered.

To her surprise, one of the blacksmiths from down the street stood just inside the doorway. She had never seen him up close before. He was usually a distant figure standing in front of the smithy. Caroline had not been aware of how largely built the man was, with thick shoulders and standing over six feet. He had short locks of black hair, a trimmed beard, and piercing blue eyes that heated her blood as though they stared directly into her soul. The packages under his flexed arm were tiny compared to the massive muscles straining the linen of his shirt.

Caroline had sworn off all men after the events at Baydon Hall, but standing so close to pure masculine power, she had trouble recollecting her commitment to abstinence as she struggled to keep her breathing even.

Except for the embedded soot around his fingernails, the man was scrupulously clean, dressed in buckskins, big black boots, a clean linen shirt, and a waistcoat. But his square face was grim. Unsmiling. He was not an exuberant man, clearly.

"So you are the new mantua-maker?" As a greeting, it was rather abrupt.

Caroline carefully prevented a crease from forming between her brows. It was only to be expected that a man—especially a tradesman—would not discern the specificities of women's fashion. To be fair, she knew little or nothing about the heating and shaping of metal to form tools. Or when steel should be used instead of iron.

As she arrived at this conclusion, Caroline gave herself a brief nod to acknowledge that she had the right of things, before beaming widely.

"There are three mantua-makers in Chatternwell. I, however, am a milliner and a modiste," she informed him proudly.

"What is the difference?"

Caroline nearly frowned, but she caught herself. "I am certain the mantua-makers are highly competent, and an integral part of the community, but the title of modiste infers a certain freshness of fashion sense. Someone knowledgeable about the latest trends. There are ladies in town who have a certain refinement of taste and elegance who require a modiste to handle their wardrobe needs."

"Aha. It allows you to sell the more expensive fabric."

"Well … yes … but … with greater profits, I am able to share my success with the seamstresses whom I employ. I pay higher wages and offer better hours."

"Are you not afraid you are stealing the livelihood from the other mantua-makers?"

Caroline smiled broadly. This was a question she could answer with confidence. "Not at all. We discovered that the more elegant ladies who are in need of a modiste have been forced to visit Bath or London for their gowns. Now they have access to the latest London designs right here in the comfort of their own town. Many households cannot afford our services, so the economies of the other shops will remain undisturbed."

"We?"

Caroline hesitated, not sure how to respond. Why had she allowed that to slip? "My business adviser, Mr. Johnson. He works for my primary investor."

If the blacksmith asked another rude question, such as who was her primary investor, she would be forced to be rude in return. She would never reveal her connection to the Earl of Saunton lest the townspeople—she suppressed a wince—drew the mostly correct conclusion.

She could not deny the frisson of irritation coursing through her veins at the gentleman's interrogation. Unfortunately, to her intense dismay, it accompanied a sensation of coiling desire. The blacksmith was annoying but handsome and intelligent, quickening her pulse as she fought to maintain her composure. A combination of frustration and titillation fired her belly … and lower.

She squashed it. It would not do.

Caroline, you wanton wench! You vowed there would be no men! Stop ogling the brute and get him out of your shop!

The blacksmith nodded. "And how does one become a modiste? You apprenticed?"

"I did. Signora Ricci serves the nobility in London and graciously taught me the details of running a fashionable merchant shop."

"The details of running a shop … Did you apprentice on millinery and dress-making somewhere else, then?"

Caroline nearly grimaced. This man was far too clever. He had caught every slip, proving she would need to prepare a better story for just such a situation if she did not wish to reveal too many details of her past. Pinning her smile in place, she gave him his answer.

"I was in service at Baydon Hall in Somerset. The house-keeper, Mrs. Harris, apprenticed me in the sewing arts."

The blacksmith frowned, tilting his head in question. "Is there much call for a seamstress in a stately home?"

"There is a surprising number of tasks. Repairs to curtains and cushions. Mending livery, mobcaps, and other household attire. In theory, I worked in the kitchen, but I mostly did needlework for my entire tenure under Mrs. Harris, who had vast experience in such things."

He drew a heavy breath. "Modiste."

It sounded as if the blacksmith was trying the word out, feeling the shape of it on his tongue. Caroline's eyes widened in shock as she imagined his tongue and— She cut the thought off before it could fully materialize.

That aspect of your life is dead and buried!

"I am William Jackson."

Caroline stepped back in surprise.

The man was not just *a* blacksmith. He was *the* black-smith, owner of the largest smithy in Chatternwell with numerous journeymen and apprentices in his employ. From what she had heard, he was an astute merchant who stocked an array of iron and steel tools, locks, and other mechanisms for purchase. Considering his accomplishments, he was rather humbly attired. Caroline supposed he might be in want of a wife to coax him into displaying his success.

She had gathered from her staff's gossip that the smithy itself rivaled the best in Bath for its excellent work. Apparently, the man had set quite a few female hearts aflutter, but had shown no sign of interest. It was surprising to meet the man and discover firsthand his lack of social finesse. It must have been his appearance and business acumen that had the women of Chatternwell so enthralled, not his fine manners.

"I need a gift for my neighbor, Mrs. Heeley. Something suitable for an old woman who does not get around much."

Now that she was no longer being interrogated, Caroline suppressed a thrill of visceral pleasure at the gruff tones of his deep voice. Mr. Jackson was pure man, and it was heady to be a petite woman in his overpowering presence. Awareness of her femininity was undeniable in such a presence. Wait … She had already thought about his powerful presence. Presence, presence, presence, thumped her heart relentlessly.

Good Lord, he is intoxicating. Whoever eventually claimed the man's attentions would be fortunate indeed.

"Of course. How about a pretty shawl to keep her warm in the winter months? We have just received a fine selection." Caroline was proud of how even her voice sounded, even if it had taken a fraction too long to respond.

Mr. Jackson raised his massive shoulders in a shrug. He was a man of few words. Caroline smiled encouragingly and steered him toward the shawls.

Fifteen minutes later, his purchase made, it was almost a relief to watch him exit the shop. The man had a physical charm that was exhausting to ignore. She wanted to fling herself against him and rub her body in wild abandon against his powerful form, which went against all her principles— she must be a chaste woman after the painful lessons of her past. Nay, she would need to keep her distance from Mr. Jackson of the rough but attractive features and virile being. She had a reputation to uphold in her adopted home.

This had been easier when she was in service. Not only

was there no time for relationships, one was not permitted to marry, which had made her vow much simpler to keep.

The man was pure temptation despite his gruff manner, and Caroline vowed to stay at her end of the street and leave Mr. Jackson to his.

CHAPTER TWO: THE REQUEST

CHRISTMAS EVE, 1820

*A*nnie finished fastening the last Christmas bough to the shop window. Turning around, she planted her small fists on her waist and declared, "There you are, Mrs. Brown! All decked out for the holidays!"

Caroline clapped her hands and smiled in acknowledgment. She did not celebrate the holidays herself, but she had commissioned Mrs. Greer to make up boughs and sprigs for the shop as an excuse to pay her some coin. It did not displease her to enjoy the aromatic greenery until Twelfth Night, when it must be taken down to avoid bad luck.

Annie had filled out in the past weeks, and Mrs. Greer's health was gradually improving, which made it all worthwhile. The child had turned out to be a hard worker, sweeping the shop, waxing the counters, and dusting the shelves with vigor. She had also begun to help with small sewing projects, and Caroline had paid Mrs. Greer for little jobs here or there that she could manage around her ailments. Caroline had wondered if the lack of funds, and subsequent poor diet, were the underlying cause of the widow's ill health.

Caroline might not be celebrating the holidays herself, but she was ensuring the Greers had the means to.

"Good work, Annie! It is very festive! Tell your mum she did a very fine job."

"It smells so good!" Annie took a deep breath, clearly enjoying the scent of rosemary, which had been woven into the bough along with holly, ivy, and Christmas rose, as the girl had loudly proclaimed when she had brought them in this morning.

Caroline grinned, giving an exaggerated sniff for her apprentice's pleasure. It smelled good, like a forest of greenery.

"I think you have done excellent work, young lady. You should go assist your mother to prepare your Christmas feast for tomorrow."

Annie's mouth immediately drooped. "Are you sure you will not join us, Mrs. Brown?"

"Do not worry about me. I have work to complete. It will be a pleasure to finish my walking dress over the next couple of days. When you come in to work on Tuesday, I shall be able to show it to you."

Caroline had gotten as close as she was willing to get to the Greers. She needed to maintain some distance, and sharing the holidays with them would be more proximity than her vow to focus on her work would bear. "Now come see your board for the week!"

She had been sending a basket of food home with Annie each week. Eggs and fresh vegetables to assist the girl and her mother with their health. She called it Annie's board because the girl not living with her was not customary for apprentices. Truthfully the wages she paid were meant to be in lieu of the room and board she would have provided if she had had a home. Referring to the basket of food that Caroline purchased from the market each week as board was an excuse to discreetly take care of the Greers while preserving their pride. It did not cost her much, and she had minimal personal expenses to worry about, but it clearly made a difference for them.

Caroline reached under the counter and pulled out the large hamper. Placing it on the counter, she beckoned the child over. "Look inside."

Annie threw a quizzical glance, then lifted the checkered cloth to peer inside. She gasped. "Is that—?"

"I included mince pies and oranges this week, and I placed an order with Mr. Andrews that you can collect after service tomorrow."

"Mr. Andrews? Which one?" Annie's forehead furrowed in confusion.

"The baker."

The girl's face reflected her amazement. "Never say, Mrs. Brown! Is it a Christmas goose?"

Caroline nodded, enjoying the evidence of Annie's joy. "For you and your mum to enjoy a proper Christmas feast."

Annie's lower lip trembled. Running around the counter, she threw her little arms around Caroline's waist in a tight embrace. "Please come eat with us, Mrs. Brown. It is not right for you to be alone over the holidays."

Caroline's stomach twinged. It would be her first Christmastide alone. As a girl, she had spent it with her grandmother, and after Grandmama had died, Caroline shared the holiday traditions with the other servants at Baydon Hall. Even last year, and the year before, she had celebrated with the doctor's household.

But she had grown too close to the Greers already. It was imperative she remain aloof to hold her secrets close. The bitter truth was that she did not deserve kinship after what she had done to Miss Annabel.

No need to think of that. Hard work will keep the memories at bay.

"Christmas is a time for family, Annie. You should be with your mum."

A muffled sniffle sounded from where Annie had her face pressed to Caroline. "You are family, Mrs. Brown."

Caroline smiled, hugging the girl before setting her away. "Go enjoy the holiday. Don't forget to fetch the goose after service tomorrow."

Annie bobbed her head, grabbing hold of the basket and struggling with the weight of it as she made to leave. "Thank you, Mrs. Brown. Merry Christmas!"

Caroline waved and then turned back to work on her account books. She was alone in the shop, it being Sunday. Mrs. Jones and Mary Beth were home preparing for their own Christmas feast.

Silence descended as Caroline scratched with her graphite pencil. Finally, she completed the accounting and put the books away under the counter. She swept her gaze around the shop with some dismay. It was so quiet, it was eerie.

The streets had been a hive of activity after services, but now there were few passersby and little noise. Shops were closed for Sabbath, and likely she was the only proprietor about. While others were home preparing for Christmas Day, she was updating the accounts to keep herself busy. The quiet brought on a sense of melancholy, and Caroline decided it was time to work on her walking dress before her memories intruded.

Walking into the back, she approached the gown that was hanging in the corner. Many months ago, on the day she had learned she was to own her shop, Caroline had purchased a fine bolt of Prussian blue velvet using her savings. She wanted to make herself a signature piece—a special walking dress with the finest sewing detail to celebrate her ascendant station in life and demonstrate her skill. She had begun sewing that very evening.

Working on it every spare minute over many hours since then, she had painstakingly stitched the shoulders, which had neat loops and whorls of fabric to create a textured and luxurious appearance. The collar was high but fell over around the neck and was richly detailed around the edge. The trimming of the robe consisted of ornate embroidery two inches wide and careful scalloping around the bottom. She had not decided about the bodice yet—an adornment of some sort would be required to complement the intricacy of the design—and the long, loose sleeves were yet to be cuffed.

When she finished, it would be the finest piece she had ever created and a testament to all her hard work over the years to achieve this level of skill.

Caroline could only hope that would fill a small part of the void in her chest which was reserved for the husband and children she would never have because of her past failures.

You threw away your chance for family when you betrayed Miss Annabel.

Caroline shook her head and reached up to remove the gown so she could begin her work. Work that brought solace to the ache within her.

* * *

WILLIAM CLOSED up the smithy and walked home to the cottages at the end of Market Street.

He had given his journeymen and apprentices time off for the holidays, and the smithy would be closed until Tuesday, the day after Christmas, except for any urgent repairs that might be needed. He had left a note on the smithy's door that he could be found at his cottage, but he was not expecting any custom from the townsfolk, so excited for the holiday festivities.

He had plans of his own. The widow next door, Mrs. Heeley, had left the day before to visit her daughter's family in Bath, so he could finally repair her roof without her knowledge.

Mrs. Heeley was a proud old woman who insisted on paying or bartering for any help William provided. Which was why, when he noticed her roof was leaking during a recent visit, William had planned to do the repairs when she left town. The widow would be none the wiser, and he could take care of her.

He had purchased slate tiles the week before, so all he needed to do was collect his tools and find his ladder. Usually, he would have an apprentice assist him with such work, but he had sent everyone home early yesterday, so they would have time to travel to their family homes for the holiday.

As he walked along the street, there were few people, except for the inn near his house, where the sound of merriment spilled out onto the deserted street. William did not mind his solitude, but the holidays always reminded him of his cousin.

They had been of an age and spent their entire youth together. After William's parents died, he had joined his cousin's family in their home. Uncle Albert had apprenticed him in the arts of the blacksmith, and he and Charles had run amok during the holidays, drinking ale and flirting with girls.

Now Charles was dead and his grieving parents had retired to Cornwall. William had taken over their smithy and thrown himself into work to bury the pain of his cousin's absence. Pain he was responsible for.

Charles would never have signed up to fight Boney's army without William's persuasion.

Since taking over the smithy, William's obsession with work had tripled the size of the business. He could keep his uncle and aunt in comfort, which was only fair considering that he had stolen their only child from their lives with his youthful indiscretion.

"It will be a lark! We shall spill French blood and protect the liberty of England!"

Young men never understood the gruesome reality of war until it was too late. He and Charles had been out of their depth, green soldiers answering the call of duty after Napoleon had escaped and raised his army anew.

William shook his head as if to fling the memories back into the recesses of his mind. Reaching Mrs. Heeley's, he walked around back to lay down the heavy tiles and went in search of his tools. Then he dug up an old ladder he kept in the back and went to lean it against the honeyed stone cottage.

Lifting the bag of tiles, he hoisted them over his shoulder and climbed. About midway up the two-story building, one of the rungs creaked in protest at his weight combined with that of the slate, and he made a mental note to avoid it on the way down.

William had not used the ladder in some time, and obviously it required attention, so he would need to take it to the smithy and repair the rung before he put it away. For now, he needed to get on with repairing the roof, as there was no telling how long it would take. He might need the next two days to complete the work, so there was no time to dillydally.

As the sun slowly set, William worked. He pulled up old tiles and threw them down into the small slip of a garden at the back. Then he fitted the replacement tiles in place. The repairs were not extensive, and he thought he could complete them today. That would free him to work on drawing up a lock design he had been contemplating. Between Christmas and Boxing Day, he might even have the time to make it and test it out.

Sitting back, he stretched his aching shoulders and looked up to enjoy the sunset.

A light flurry of snow descended from the heavens as he took in the picturesque view. The slate roofs, and chimneys bellowing cheerful smoke, gave way to rolling hills blanketed in the colors of winter, while the sky glowered a moody iron gray in the gathering darkness.

To the west, the sun emanated a weak, yellow light as it dipped over the horizon and recalled to his mind the last time he had sat on a roof like this with his cousin at his side.

It had been the year of 1815, mere weeks before they had signed up to fight Boney on the Continent.

Charles was a year younger than him and several inches shorter, but he and William could have been brothers for their similarity in coloring and physical bearing. His cousin, who had followed William into every ill-conceived situation, had spoken of how he planned to marry the lass he was courting, now that the cousins were both journeymen in their own right.

They had been next door, repairing Uncle Albert's roof after a violent storm. William could almost feel the presence of his cousin at his side now, remembering how they had discussed their hopes and dreams for the future. They pondered over the women they might marry, laughing about the rambunctious children they might have, given their misspent youth, and one day sharing the smithy as business partners when Uncle Albert retired.

William closed his eyes, willing the memory away.

Charles had been dead these five years because of William's persuasion, and only work buried the pain of that loss and guilt.

When he opened his lids once more, he realized the snow was coming down harder. It was time to go home and occupy himself with drawing the lock. The work would help him keep his memories at bay. It was simply the holidays making him sentimental. If he felt lonely running his smithy, he had only himself to blame for persuading Charles to go to war, or else his cousin would still be here to work with him.

William put his tools away in the battered valise he brought them in and gingerly made his way back to the ladder. Snowflakes were melting as they hit the slate tiles that had been warmed in the afternoon sun, causing water to slick the roof. Fortunately, his work on the roof was now done, because if the snow continued, doing repairs on Christmas Day would have been impossible.

He carefully put his foot on the wooden ladder and began his descent.

When he reached the midway point, about the height of a second floor, a loud crack echoed against the walls of the stone cottages, and William felt the forgotten rung give out under his boot.

Blazes!

William fell, his ankle caught in the ladder which fell with him as he hit the ground hard on his back, knocking the air right out of his lungs.

* * *

WHEN CAROLINE LOOKED up from her embroidery, it was to find that the light from the back window had failed. The sun was setting, and snow was falling, casting the room in a gray light.

Her shop was located amongst other merchants, so the world was absolutely quiet.

Too quiet.

A cloak of melancholy descended, so that she felt as gray as the interior of her shop.

Caroline put the walking dress down on the worktable and scolded herself.

It's the holidays. Cheer up, Caroline!

Resolutely, she stood up and began to hum the verses she and her grandmother would sing at this time of the year. Checking the back door, she locked it up before walking about the workroom. She lit every candle and lantern in the room to chase the shadows away.

Drawing a deep breath, Caroline broke into song to fill the dreary silence.

> *While shepherds watched their flocks by night,*
> *all seated on the ground,*
> *an angel of the Lord came down,*
> *and glory shone around.*

Caroline walked to the front of the shop and proceeded to light it up. As the gloom was washed away, her spirits lifted. She had many blessings.

Her walking dress would soon be finished, a priceless garment of the highest quality.

Her seamstresses were doing excellent work, and the shop's reputation was growing.

Her shop was receiving orders from the finest citizens of the town.

Mr. Johnson's recent visit had confirmed that her business was proceeding precisely as he had projected it would when he recommended the promising location in Chatternwell.

Little Annie Greer was the picture of health, and her mum was improving.

> *'Fear not,' said he, for mighty dread*
> *had seized their troubled mind;*
> *'glad tidings of great joy I bring*
> *to you and all mankind.*

And she had not strayed since that time with Lord Saunton, so she had mended her ruinous ways and stayed away from men as she had vowed to do after her horrible betrayal of Miss Annabel.

> *'To you, in David's town, this day*
> *is born of David's line*
> *a Savior, who is Christ the Lord;*
> *and this shall be the sign:*

She might be alone on Christmas Eve, but she had a whole new life to celebrate. Considering she was all alone, she could sing the song as loudly as she liked in the privacy of her closed shop.

> *'The heavenly Babe you there shall find*
> *to human view displayed,*
> *all meanly wrapped in swathing bands,*
> *and in a manger laid.'*

Caroline returned to the back room to prepare tea. While the water boiled, she found the biscuits she had purchased earlier that day at Mr. Andrews's bakery and laid some out on a plate. She should return to her rooms for dinner, but the landlady had left to visit family in Bath. The idea of being alone in the empty house instead of her fine shop seemed too depressing a prospect.

> *Thus spoke the angel. Suddenly*
> *appeared a shining throng*
> *of angels praising God, who thus*
> *addressed their joyful song:*

And the community here in Chatternwell had accepted her with open arms—that was another blessing she had not counted yet!

Raising her voice, she sang the last verse loudly as she set out her teacup. Her loneliness was a choice. A penance for her past mistakes. She had acquired many fine acquaintances here in town, and her work was all she needed.

> *'All glory be to God on high,*
> *and to the earth be peace;*
> *to those on whom his favor rests*
> *goodwill shall never cease.'*

Silence descended once more. Biting her lip, she tried to think of something else to sing. Opening her mouth, she—

A loud knocking resounded from the front door. Caroline's mouth clamped shut as she frowned in confusion.

Who on earth—

Another loud knocking.

Whoever it was, they were frantic to get her attention. The very windows rattled from the blows on the door.

Caroline briskly strode across the workroom to enter the front of the shop, more than a little nervous at whom she might find at her door on Christmas Eve. Her fears were eased when she saw through the windows that it was Dr. Hadley, one of the town's two doctors. He was a jovial sort, and quite popular for his generous spirit.

Hurrying over, Caroline unlocked the door to let him in.

Dr. Hadley was a well-fed man of average height with salt and pepper hair. He had a broad face with a thick mustache and a vaguely Mediterranean look about him. Currently, he looked harried rather than his usual cheerful self.

"Is everything all right, Dr. Hadley?"

His gravelly voice revealed his anxiety. "Mrs. Brown, I am so pleased to find you. I swear the entire street is deserted for the eve celebrations. I could not find a single soul of any use!"

"Are you in need of assistance?"

The doctor swiped a white handkerchief over his forehead, mopping up the sweat of his exertions. "I hate to impose, Mrs. Brown. There were people about when I was called to Mr. Jackson's, but by the time I was done treating him, I could find no one to help. John Bow is here to drive me urgently to his farm so I can attend to his wife. She is in labor and needs me right away, but I must find someone to take care of Mr. Jackson before I leave."

"What happened to Mr. Jackson?"

"He suffered a severe sprain to his ankle this evening. It is imperative he remain off his feet, but there is no one to care for him. The man is pugnacious! Stubborn! If I do not find someone to attend him, I know he will walk about, which could result in a permanent injury. I must send someone over to ensure he is taken care of. His last meal was at midday, so if I do not send someone to see to him right away, he is certain to ignore my instructions to remain seated and instead seek sustenance."

Caroline drew back in disbelief at what the doctor was suggesting. "Surely ... I cannot, Dr. Hadley! I am a single woman. If I attend to a man in his home, my reputation will be utterly ruined!"

And I have been avoiding the handsome blacksmith since the day we met! I cannot possibly be alone with him!

The doctor looked about, then back at the wagon where Mr. Bow sat with a tense expression, evidently concerned at the delay returning to his wife's side.

Leaning in, Dr. Hadley lowered his voice. "I shall be the only one who knows, and I swear I shall never breathe a word of it. I found a couple of people at the inn, but they were far too inebriated to be of use, and the innkeeper … he refused to help. Not that I would trust that man to care for anyone at the best of times. Everyone else is home with their family, and I do not have time to find someone else."

Caroline shook her head. She wanted to assist, but this was too risky.

"Mrs. Brown, Mr. Jackson is a very important member of our community. Under ordinary circumstances, I could find any number of people willing to assist him. And he has many staff. But it is the holidays and I am out of time. Please, this is important! I have seen injuries like this become incurable maladies due to neglect. The patient must remain off his feet. Mr. Jackson is yet a young man, a man who provides many people with work and is himself a highly skilled smith who helps our community by his own hand. I would hate for him to develop chronic problems with his leg when he was doing such a kind favor."

"Dr. Hadley, if someone sees me entering his home, it could ruin my business. I would be run out of town."

The doctor reached out, clasping her hand gently in his own to stare deep into her eyes. "Mrs. Brown, I assure you it is the right thing to do. You can approach the house from the alley and enter through his back door. Mrs. Bow is having her first child, and I must get to her side immediately. I know it is a lot to ask …"

Caroline rubbed her free hand over her chin. She looked

out on the deserted street. Hers was the only light to be seen, which was evidently how the doctor had found her. It could not do any harm. No one was about to see. As long as she was discreet, she could help the doctor, and she did not have a good reason to refuse her help. Hesitantly, she nodded.

Dr. Hadley squeezed her hand in gratitude. "Thank you, Mrs. Brown. His cottage is near the end of the street, just past Mrs. Heeley's. You will know you have reached her house by the broken tiles and ladder in her backyard. If you can just take care of him until tomorrow night, I swear to it that no one will ever know you were there!"

The doctor dug in his pocket, pulling out a page and thrusting it into her hand. "Here are my instructions for Mr. Jackson's care. I will call on him on Tuesday morning and bring one of his apprentices along to take care of him then."

With that, Dr. Hadley turned to run over to the wagon, his great wool coat flapping in the night air as he hastily raised himself onto the seat next to Mr. Bow.

The farmer tipped his hat in greeting to Caroline, then prompted his horse forward. She watched as they started down the street through the falling snow, hoping that John Bow was oblivious to the specifics of the doctor's request or there would be too many people aware of where she was going tonight.

Locking the door, she read the doctor's scrawling handwriting as she considered what she might need to take with her. Making a mental list, she gathered her things, put out the candles, and headed to the back to find her cloak. She suspected it would be a long night, what with her and the blacksmith spending Christmas Eve together.

Alone.

Was the universe throwing temptation in her path to test her will? Certainly by morning she would know if she had managed to transform herself into a chaste woman these past two years since her ill-advised indiscretions with Lord Saunton in the stables.

CHAPTER THREE: THE INVASION

*W*illiam woke from a doze, shaking his head to clear the fog. His ankle was thrumming something fierce. He supposed the dull ache might be the cause of his fatigue, sapping his energy.

His front room was dark except for the glow of the fire which was dying out. He would be without light soon.

William sat up, setting off sharp twinges in his leg. Dr. Hadley had instructed him to recline on the settee and rest, promising to send over someone to assist him, but the doctor must have failed to locate anyone. William would need to get up and take care of himself.

He attempted to stand, then dropped back down with a torrent of expletives. Huffing a deep sigh, he tried to think what to do. The fire needed to be stoked, and he needed to eat if he was to maintain his strength, but his ankle was a fiery throb and Dr. Hadley's admonition had been that he would take far longer to heal if he failed to stay off his feet.

It is obvious the doctor is not going to find someone willing to attend me on Christmas Eve.

For the first time, William considered if his life choices

were questionable. He might have built a successful smithy, but he had no family and no close friends. Now he sat injured during the holidays without a solitary person to assist him. Not one person was thinking of him this evening.

His stomach growled, as if to contribute its sentiments to the conversation he was having with himself.

With a loud groan, William fell back onto the settee and raised his legs back onto the arm. He would rise and take care of the fire and find a meal in his kitchen, but he just wanted to lie back and scowl at the ceiling.

Slowly he drifted off, when the click of a door handle had his eyes flying back open. He heard the scrape of his back door opening and the sound of footsteps on the stone floor of his kitchen.

Someone huffed with exertion, followed by the sound of something heavy hitting the oak table where he ate his meals. William frowned. The doctor had found someone to send over?

Was it one of the boys who lived in the cottage on the next street? Surely, it was not any of the men from the inn nearby. William muttered under his breath at this thought. Was his nocturnal visitor inebriated? The doctor had better sense than that … he hoped.

From the back, he could hear a candle being lit, a low glow of light seeping in through the doorway.

"Mr. Jackson?"

William struggled back up to a seated position, surprise causing his heart to beat like a drum. It was a woman! But who …

Oh, no! No, no, no … Please, Lord, assure me the doctor did not send—

"Mr. Jackson?"

It was her! Bathed in the light of the candle, she held a candleholder in her hand. The glow accentuated her blonde hair, casting her lovely face in attractive shadows and casting light on her delightful, rounded bosom. The woman he had been avoiding these past weeks now stood in his home, like a little ray of sunshine peeking through glowering clouds.

So much for maintaining my distance!

"Dr. Hadley sent me to tend to you. He said you are injured?"

William shook his head in dismay, stroking his beard while he tried to think. "You cannot be here!"

Mrs. Brown ignored him, walking around the room to light more candles before setting down her candleholder and taking up the fire poker to bank the fire. William watched, helpless, while savoring the cheeriness that she brought with her.

"Dr. Hadley impressed upon me the importance of your health to our little community, and assured me that no one would learn of my presence. Do you know that the lock on your back door is broken? It does not catch properly."

She came forward to stand before him. William scowled. "What on earth are you wearing?"

He could hear his tone was barking, but he could not help it. Shock at her proximity, the woman who had been disturbing his mind since their meeting the month before, warred with the pain in his leg and the impulse to maintain the privacy of his home. She was not just attractive; she was a force to be reckoned with as a single woman who had launched a successful shop in an unfamiliar town and already made her mark. His fellow proprietors were speaking of her incessantly, which made it all the more difficult to push her out of his thoughts. Having her in such close proximity was dangerous to his state of emotionless equilibrium.

Mrs. Brown looked down at her cloak. "It is a winter cloak."

41

"It is decidedly not! There is no possibility that cloak keeps you warm in the winter. Why does it have such wide sleeves? There is nothing to prevent the chill!"

Mrs. Brown wrinkled her nose, an expression of irritation dancing across her features. "It is beautiful and I love it! I made it from the remnants of a coat my grandmother owned ... After she died."

The last was said with a sad intonation, and William experienced a gouging guilt. That was the problem with Mrs. Brown. She made him feel things. Heaving an exasperated breath, he relented. "I apologize. Show it to me."

The modiste brightened up, mercurial in her shift of mood. "I made it from green velvet and cut up my grandmother's coat to create this fur trimming." She turned the lapel to show him the pale pelt that framed the velvet.

"And what of the sleeves?" The utterly impractical sleeves that could not possibly assist with the retention of heat on a cold winter night?

Mrs. Brown held up one of her arms to display the deep fall of the sleeve. "I saw something like it in a woodcutting of a woman in a medieval gown. It appealed to my romantic side."

"Let me see it, then."

She twirled, and despite how odd and useless the garment was, William had to admit she looked ravishing in the dark green velvet and pale fur with the wide hood framing her face.

Mrs. Brown was a personification of Christmas, and when she came to a stop, his eyes once more came to rest on her lovely mouth that had haunted his thoughts these past weeks. Despite his discomfort, he briefly imagined standing up to sweep her into his arms and plant a kiss on those wide, pink lips.

Mrs. Brown frowned, apparently noticing something odd

about his expression. "Mr. Jackson, I must insist you lie back down and rest as the doctor instructed."

Soughing, he shifted and settled back against the settee's arm, stretching out his legs once more. He would never state it aloud, but it was gratifying to raise his leg, which diminished the persistent throbbing.

"Your cloak is lovely," he admitted roughly. "But, Mrs. Brown, I need your assurance that you would not venture out into a serious cold snap with such a garment. The cold would find no difficulty in chilling you to the bone with such gaping cuffs."

Mrs. Brown snorted a low laugh. "I work all the time, and then race home to my rooms. There is no possibility of my freezing out in the cold."

"Nevertheless, Mrs. Brown—"

"If we are to spend Christmas together, perhaps it would be easier to call me Caroline?"

William's breath stopped in his lungs for the span of a second before he rebuked himself to take air.

Caroline.

It was wondrously fitting for such an exquisite and accomplished woman.

After several seconds of silence, he realized Mrs. Br— Caroline was gazing at him expectantly.

"You may call me William."

This was going to be a very long night. Caroline's presence heated his blood and made him desire her nearness. He wondered what it might feel like to hold her soft body in his arms. What she might smell of.

That thought was torturous!

Now all he could think of was to pull her down onto the settee with him so he might bury his face in her pretty flaxen hair to discover her unique scent.

William exhaled deeply in agitation.

43

"How did you injure yourself ... William?"

There was a hesitancy to how she formed his name on her lips. William shot her a glance, observing how her eyes skittered away, and he realized the young woman was as nervous as he at this unexpected interlude of theirs.

"It was nothing. Just a mishap with my ladder. I spend little time at home, so my tools here are not well maintained like the ones in the smithy. It turned out to be a mistake to use them without inspection."

"Huh. So nothing to do with the roof repairs at Mrs. Heeley's cottage?"

William scowled. She was too damned observant. "How did you know that?"

"I saw the broken ladder and tiles out back. It was very kind of you to help the widow. Did she ask you to take care of it on Christmas Eve for a particular reason? Would it not have been easier with the help of one of your men?"

William mumbled his reply in a resentful tone.

"What was that?"

He frowned before admitting the truth in a louder voice. "Mrs. Heeley didn't ask. You are not to mention it to her. I need to have one of my apprentices clean up the clutter so she will not learn of it, or it will embarrass her that I interceded."

"You secretly repaired her roof on Christmas Eve?" William heard the note of awed admiration in Caroline's voice, which stirred a visceral warmth in his lower belly, close to the region of his—

No, William!

They might be spending the holidays together, but there was no reason to become too intimate in their conversation. He admired her far too much already, so he needed to avoid finding ever more traits to attract him further to the young woman.

Tearing his eyes from her, he scowled at the ceiling. "Are you going to make something to eat, or what?"

A melodic chuckle was her only response. William listened as her feet pattered out of the room, the urge to call her back almost overpowering. Almost.

* * *

CAROLINE CHUCKLED as she made her way back to the kitchen. The blacksmith might be grim and full of bluster, but he had just revealed his soft side. He had injured himself doing secret repairs for the old woman next door. Mr. Jacks —William was kind under all that cantankerous posturing.

She had to admit to her relief that the man was on his back. William was far less imposing now that he was not towering over her, a wall of muscle and sinews that beat iron and steel into shape for his livelihood.

William. It suited him. A strong English name for a strong English man.

She could not deny a frisson of awareness that was running through her veins, but given that the man was relegated to lying on his back, she was confident she could maintain her equilibrium. All she had to do was get through the night without incident, and she would know that she had found her footing—and moral backbone—around handsome men.

Granted, William was nowhere near as charming as Lord Saunton, the man who proved her errant character, but he was just as virile. If not more so. Caroline could test her mettle. Fortunately, the man was laid up, so he posed little risk.

Humming a Christmas carol, she put water to boil. Scrounging around the kitchen, she located his tea things and decided to make the blacksmith a sandwich. She would make him something more robust in the morning, but tonight it would be best to feed him as speedily as possible.

She cut the fresh bread she had found, adding slices of cheese and smoked ham, then laid it out on a plate. Then she cut a much smaller sandwich for herself. Digging through her basket, she located the biscuits from Mr. Andrews, laying out York biscuits alongside rolled wafers. She doubted that a man such as William would wish to have milk in his tea, so she poured two cups, leaving his untouched while adding a little milk to her own.

Picking up the laden tray, and still humming her Christmas tune, Caroline walked back to the sitting room.

William was laid out on the settee, his eyes shut. Now that there was more light in the room, Caroline noted a pallor to his bronzed skin. The man clearly needed to eat.

Walking over, she placed the tray down on the table between the settees before taking a seat across from him. William slowly opened his eyes, his blue gaze finding the tray, and an expression of raw hunger flashed across his face. He pushed himself up to lean against the arm of the settee, his stomach growling loudly as if the proximity of the food had awakened a tiger.

"Thank you ... Caroline."

The sound of her name on his lips caused a delicious shiver to travel from her nape down her spine. William had sculpted, smooth lips—something she could not help noticing on the day they had met—and she guessed instinctively that they would be warm to the touch.

There will be no touching, Caroline!

Her eyelids flickered as she chased the musings from her wayward thoughts. Lifting the plate with his thick-cut sandwich, she handed it over with a nod of acknowledgment, then moved his teacup so he could reach it.

She picked up her own tea to sip, lifting her sandwich to

take a bite before setting it back down. Peeking from beneath her eyelashes, she observed him devouring his sandwich. Picking up his tea, he sipped the scalding liquid rather fast. She supposed as a blacksmith, he was more accustomed to high heats than herself. With satisfaction, she watched his color return to normal as he consumed his dinner.

Now that she was finally off her feet, Caroline swung her head to look about the room. Above the fireplace hung a seascape of a calm day on the water with tiny boats bobbing under the bright sun while waves crashed onto the rocks at the foot of a cliff. Between the comfortable, overstuffed settees lay a rug woven in blues and greens, and several plump pillows in similar hues decorated them. And across the room, tucked in the corner next to the staircase, was a small wooden table and four chairs with matching seat cushions.

"Your cottage is not what I expected."

William swung his head up from eating his sandwich, shrugging his broad shoulders and setting off a quiver in her, which she quickly suppressed. "I have not redecorated it since I took it over. Aunt Gertrude is from Cornwall."

He gestured to the painting.

"I like it," she assured him before continuing her meal.

After taking several bites of her own sandwich, she finally stood. Taking his teacup to refill it, she went back to the kitchen. Returning to William, she found him chewing on a York biscuit with an expression of bliss. He nodded his thanks when she placed the cup down. The biscuit looked small and inconsequential in his powerful hand, which brought up notions of—

No, Caroline!

Chastised, she retreated to the kitchen. With determination, she took up the supplies she had brought and returned to the front room to grab one of the chairs in the corner and drag it to the windows.

"What are you doing?"

"I am making your home festive."

"You brought Christmas boughs to attend to me?" The man appeared genuinely perplexed as Caroline sat down with the boughs in her lap and began to tie one to the windowsill.

"Why not? We are stuck together for Christmas, and there is no one at my shop to appreciate these. They are wonderful, are they not? Mrs. Greer made them for me." Caroline breathed deeply of the rosemary scent as she worked. She did not miss the quizzical look William threw in her direction. He clearly thought she was a madwoman, bedecking his home. But if work kept her mind busy and prevented her imagination from straying in unwanted directions, then William was going to have the most festive home in all of Chatternwell.

Blazes, he is a handsome man!

Not like Lord Saunton, one of the handsomest men she had ever laid eyes on. Nay, William Jackson was handsome in a masculine, roughly hewn manner that made her think of hot, sweaty activities that she was avoiding. His body was obviously powerful beneath the thin disguise of minimal clothing, his muscles well developed from thousands of hours of pounding metal and working bellows. Currently, his white shirt gaped open to reveal the column of his neck. His waistcoat had been divested, and he wore only one stocking, with one hairy, muscled calf on display.

It is simply a test, Caroline! You are to prove you have matured into a chaste woman!

She cleared her throat and hummed another carol while her fingers worked on the boughs. What a relief that she had brought something to do! Even now she could feel his eyes following her, but once she was done with this, she had more work to do. She would prepare a poultice for his sprain following the doctor's directions, then clean up the kitchen. If she was clever, she could keep herself occupied until the blacksmith fell asleep.

Caroline's eyes widened in horror, and her humming halted. She had not considered where she would be sleeping later tonight. The blacksmith would likely remain on the settee because the flight of stairs was both narrow and steep. With the state of his swollen leg, he would not make it up the steps.

She supposed she could sleep in his bed on the next floor, a thought that shot a riot of tingling sensation over her, but she might not hear if he called for help.

Biting her lip, she glanced around the sitting room, her fingers ceasing to work until she glimpsed the second settee. It was large enough for her to rest.

Across the room, William followed her gaze and, for the first time since she met him, a smile spread across his face. It was devastating—a slash of white teeth startling in contrast to his dark beard—and Caroline found herself struggling for breath as she focused on the lips she had noticed before.

"You are wondering where you will sleep?"

Speechless, her tongue tied by her lustful imaginings, all she could do was nod.

"Perhaps before you decide that, you might want to draw the drapes." He gestured to the window where she was working. Stricken, Caroline spun her head round to stare out at the deserted street in dismay. She could only hope no one had walked by. Standing in haste, Christmas boughs falling to the floor, she jerked the blue curtains shut and then ran to the other window to shut those, too.

There she stood, panting in panic as she stared at the drapes.

"No one saw you." William's husky voice broke the silence.

"Are you certain?"

"I am. I have had a clear view of the windows since you walked within view. Caroline … I want you to know that if any of this damages your reputation … I would do the right thing."

Caroline stopped breathing. That was the last thing she needed to hear. In all her years on this earth, no man had ever offered such a thing. Even if it was merely to protect her reputation, it was still … noble.

The attractive blacksmith, who secretly took care of old ladies, was now offering to be a gentleman and marry her in the event her reputation suffered? She did not need to admire the man any more than she already did. Or imagine lying in the marriage bed with him leaning over her.

"You want to … marry me?"

Several seconds passed, wood crackling in the fireplace the only sound in the silence. Finally, he replied, his reluctance evident. "I would prefer not to marry, but if it was required, we could come to an arrangement."

Caroline slowly resumed breathing. "I … appreciate it. But as you said, no one was out there to witness my presence."

* * *

HAD he just offered to marry the woman? William shook his head after Caroline left the room, mumbling about preparing a poultice.

He supposed he would do it if he had to because he could not possibly leave a fine woman of Caroline's quality to suffer for doing him a good deed. He could not allow it for a woman of any quality, but especially not the lovely mantua-maker who had impressed many of his acquaintances with her keen business sense.

Modiste.

William shook his head at the self-admonishment. Life was taking unexpected turns since he had noticed Caroline beckoning Annie Greer into her shop. He would never have thought to understand the difference between the two types of dressmakers, yet here he was discerning it.

From the kitchen, he heard Caroline begin to hum again. The melody was relaxing, and he was happy to hear she was once more returned to her cheerful self. Her alarm at noticing the curtains were open had been momentarily amusing, but as her disquiet became obvious, he had realized the serious repercussions for a young woman to be seen at his home alone. Men did not have to concern themselves over such things, but a young proprietress such as Caroline, who had just begun her first business, would be utterly ruined socially and likely financially, too.

William lay back and shut his eyes, listening with mild enjoyment to Caroline preparing the poultice for his ankle. The holidays alone had always been daunting, which was why he busied himself with work in the festive season. Being laid up like this would be sheer torture to his now idle mind, so having company in the house was a boon to his soul. A distraction from the dark memories.

It would be acceptable to allow it for just a night or two.

When Caroline returned, she had the poultice on a tray, which she set down on the low table before taking a seat on the sturdy furnishing. The doctor had removed his stocking when he had bound up William's ankle. She now carefully unwound the bandage, humming to herself. It was something that had struck him about the modiste. She always seemed cheerful.

"I am sorry you have to spend your holidays nursing me."

Caroline's hazel eyes found his. "It is quite all right, William. I was working, as it happened."

A smile of gratitude flickered across his lips, but it saddened him to think that a lovely woman such as Caroline was spending Christmas Eve alone. She should have a husband and a bevy of children at her side. The way she had taken care of Annie Greer, despite being new to town, spoke to the goodness residing in her heart.

Caroline wrinkled her nose as she washed the swelling with warm vinegar. Then she applied the compress to his leg. "My word, the spirits in this mixture are strong! Quite enough to take one's breath away!"

William gritted his teeth at the sense of helplessness to be tended to like a child, mingled with the enjoyment of her delicate fingers pressing against him. "What is it?"

"The poultice? The doctor instructed a variety of ingredients. Vinegar, oatmeal, camphorated spirits of wine, Mindererus's spirit, volatile liniment, volatile aromatic spirit diluted with a double quantity of water, and the common fomentation, with the addition of brandy."

"My word, did I have all those ingredients?"

She smiled. "No, I only found four or five. Hopefully, it will do."

"I am sure it will. Dr. Hadley seemed to think the key measure was to rest the leg. He had me soak it in ice water when he first arrived."

"There you go, then. We will use the poultice and then I will bind it to your ankle. By the time Christmastide is over, you will hopefully be mostly healed."

"Are you always such an optimist?"

Her hands stilled in their task, and William got the sense that Caroline was thinking of unpleasant things before she finally replied. "I find it is important to count one's blessings.

The world can be very lonely, but if you take the time to count your blessings, you can be happier."

"What blessings would you count for me tonight? Now that I have sprained my ankle in this stupid manner." He waved his hand toward his leg.

"You are a well-respected blacksmith with a successful business. The doctor respects and admires you, so he took great pains to find an attendant to be at your side. You are strong and healthy, which means if you follow his directions, you should be fully recovered within a few days. And ... you have your entire life ahead of you!"

As Caroline completed her litany of blessings, the glow of her face captivated William. Her lively hazel eyes were brimming with sincere interest. She meant it, speaking with conviction. It gave him pause to hear his situation described by the woman who embodied sheer sunshine in his mind.

A fire sprang to life in his belly as he watched her, the urge to reach out and pull her into his arms a physical impulse he had to quell.

Careful, William. You are feeling things. Feelings lead to loss and pain. Feelings nearly broke you when Charles died.

With more force than he intended, before the sunshine could spread into the recesses of his soul to reawaken his dead spirits, William bit back, "Are you nearly done?"

Caroline flinched as if he had slapped her instead of rejected her blessings. The crestfallen look that followed stabbed him deep in the chest, and William feared that he had taken action too late. The withered organ that lay in his breast had already begun its slow return to life.

"I shall bind the poultice to your ankle when I am done clearing up."

With that, Caroline stood up and left the room. William squashed any burgeoning guilt. They had at least tonight and perhaps another day of each other's company, and it was essential he maintain some distance. It would not do to get ideas about spending time together. As it was, his earlier offer had put images of courtship in his head, and that was an impossibility.

William recalled how, when he had returned home, he had had to tell his Uncle Albert and Aunt Gertrude that their only child was dead, without even a proper burial on foreign soil.

All because of him, because of his selfish desires.

After contending with their heartrending grief, his news destroying their very light, he had to inform Charles's betrothed on the other side of the village. Nellie had shattered into pieces in his arms. She had mourned for the longest time until she finally met a man in Bath just a year ago and finally healed.

William had caused far too much unhappiness in his past to consider embracing sunshine in his future.

Nay, he had all but died at the Hougoumont farmhouse along with Charles, and he was not permitted to return to life.

To his relief, Caroline worked in the kitchen without her usual humming in accompaniment. Listening to her earlier had tugged at strange yearnings, and William wanted none of it. Sunshine needed to be kept at bay. It was his lot to live in shadows.

Before long, she returned clothed in a night rail and wrap, which was embroidered with neat, little flowers. Her work, perhaps? Silky hair was plaited to fall over her shoulder, and his fingers itched to pull on the primrose ribbon and comb through her wheat locks.

Sitting on the low table, Caroline bound the poultice, her fingers warm on his leg, then spread a blanket over him. It was only midevening, but his eyelids were heavy and he was more than ready to slumber.

Despite this, William's eyes could not help themselves. They devoured the shape of her with hunger as she wandered about, quietly extinguishing the candles in the darkening room.

When she finally reclined on the opposite settee, William's lids shut and he accepted the gentle embrace of sleep.

CHAPTER FOUR: THE PAST

*W*illiam opened his eyes to find himself once more at Château d'Hougoumont.

It was right about noon, with the sun beating down on the quagmire of mud left in the rainstorm's wake earlier that morning, when the north gate was breached. A sous-lieutenant of the French First Light Infantry broke through the gate with an axe, enabling blue-coats to pour into the fortified courtyard that William's regiment had been charged with defending.

William frantically sought his cousin's position, yelling his name, when he caught sight of Charles near the gate. From thirty feet away, William raced forward to assist him, but he was too late. He could only watch helplessly as Charles was run through with a flashing steel bayonet, falling to the ground as if time itself had slowed down to drag out William's agonizing futility.

For the span of a second, William was frozen as grief slammed into his body, almost bringing him to his knees. Even at this distance, there was no doubt his cousin was dead, with his empty eyes staring into the abyss.

But then there was no time to think as the tide of French soldiers reached him. Realizing there was no time to reload his musket, he raised it up to fight, as he had been taught weeks ago when Charles and he had signed up to fight Boney. Which was when he noticed that his bayonet was missing. William saw the soldiers were upon him, and he had no method to defend himself.

Recalling the training sergeant had said that Brown Bess had a thick stock and would not break if he used it as a club, William's instincts as a blacksmith spurred him into motion while a mindless rage washed over him in a tide of red. They had killed his cousin, his best friend. If he were to die in the yard today, he would take as many Frenchmen down with him as he could!

William raised his musket like a forge hammer, swinging it down with the force and precision of a smith beating iron on his anvil. Cracking it down, he raised it once more and swung it down. And raised it and swung again. And again.

When William's rage slowly dissipated, he was panting from his exertions. He groggily returned to his senses from the anger and hatred that had engulfed his mind, to find that he now stood with five dead Frenchmen at his feet. The north gate was closed, and his fellow red-coats were frantically fighting the remaining enemy left within the yard.

It was like this every night. Every relentless night since the battle of Waterloo.

This was the part of his recurring nightmare when he threw back his head to roar all the pain, and loss, and regret shuddering through him. Charles was dead, and William had killed five men in close combat with the skills of his livelihood turned to abhorrent violence. He did not even know the men's names. Would never know their names. Or if they had wives, children, parents who would grieve them.

This was the precise moment he would now make his vow to—
Then he heard it, a melodic voice humming a Christmas carol.

> *Thus spoke the angel. Suddenly*
> *appeared a shining throng*

57

> of angels praising God, who thus
> addressed their joyful song:
>
> 'All glory be to God on high,
> and to the earth be peace;
> to those on whom his favor rests
> goodwill shall never cease.'

He frowned, hesitating, uncertain of what to make of the joyful holiday song here in this yard of death.

This was a fresh development. He had suffered this nightmare for more than five years. It had never deviated before. Every night, it was the same sequence of events. Over and over again, so that he was afraid to fall asleep. Afraid to revisit this yard.

William shook his head in befuddlement, then turned to discover the source of the song.

Approaching him was sunshine herself, draped in a flowing white gown. Her blonde hair was lit, her face serene as she walked toward him, paying no mind to the carnage at her feet. She sang as she neared him, and somehow the soldiers parted to let her through so she might come to a stop in front of him.

Caroline Brown looked up into his eyes and asked, "Did you count your blessings, William?"

"Blessings?" he echoed dumbly.

She shook her head at him, as if admonishing a forgetful child. "Life is hard. Counting your blessings makes it easier to find happiness in this world."

His brow creased, and he found himself at a genuine loss as he stared down at his filthy breeches and muddy boots, while breathing in the stench of blood and gunpowder. Surely this was a jest? There was no possibility of hope or optimism to be found in a hell like this. Caroline could not possibly have any blessings of value to share with him.

"What blessings are to be found in this field of death?"

Her pink lips curled into a smile, and William wondered if he was missing some vital clue. She seemed confident there was grace present. "There are always blessings to be counted. It is all about perspective."

She held out a hand, and it was clean. And soft. And perfect. He did not wish to sully her by taking hold of it, but she merely stood there, waiting with a tilt of her head until he reluctantly reached out to clasp it. "Come with me, blacksmith."

Leading him over to a fortified wall, she stepped up onto a barrel with his help, then gestured for him to take his place at her side. Gingerly, he climbed up and turned to where she was peering with a fascinated expression.

William's eyes widened in amazement as he realized he was watching himself. Events unfolded once more, but this time he watched them from the side. He was no longer a participant in the battle.

The French sous-lieutenant broke through the north gate, wielding his steel axe in a triumphant charge.

Blue-coats followed him, flooding into the courtyard.

William watched once more in torment as Charles was run through with a bayonet, this vantage point a fresh seat to witness hell unfolding yet again.

Then William watched himself across the yard as he called out his cousin's name in agony. He witnessed the other William's anguish, followed by the realization he had no bayonet with which to defend himself as the tide of blue rushed toward him. The other William brought the musket back over his head to wield it in the manner of a blacksmith's hammer.

Caroline was humming next to him, nudging him and pointing to the left of where William was fighting the enemy.

Curious what had her attention, he focused on where she pointed and noticed for the first time that as he fought, Corporal Graham, Graham's brother, and several soldiers were fighting near him while Captain Wyndham led them to the north gate. As the other William brought the stock of his musket down on the head of a French soldier, he now noticed that the man had been preparing to stab Corporal Graham from behind with the point of his bayonet.

The corporal paid no heed to what was happening behind him as William cracked his stock down on the French soldier's head, killing him in a single, powerful blow. Graham raised his musket and fired at a French sniper who was taking aim at Captain Wyndham. He hit the sniper and then the group of red-coats fought their way forward under the command of Lieutenant Colonel MacDonell to the north gate. Closing the gate was their only hope of survival, and the men fought their way valiantly in service of the British army, as they had been instructed to do. Château d'Hougoumont had to be defended at any cost.

William watched on, realizing for the first time that while he fought in the skirmish across the yard, his fellow red-coats made it back to the gate and struggled to get it closed. Then they turned to fight the remaining blue-coats in the yard.

Caroline broke off from her song. "If you had not been standing in that exact spot, Corporal Graham might have died. If he had died, so too would Captain Wyndham have died. And if Captain Wyndham had died, Lieutenant Colonel MacDonell would have failed and Hougoumont would have fallen."

"What of it?" William heard the belligerence in his voice, but he could not help it. He had returned to the site of his downfall as he did every horrible night. It was hell on earth, and he had had to relive it every night since that day.

Caroline turned to gaze at him with lively hazel eyes. "It was a blessing you were here that day, William. The Duke of Wellington himself declared that the success of the battle turned upon the closing of the gates at Hougoumont."

William's brows drew together in his confusion. He supposed he must have known that, considering Caroline was merely a guest in his dream. She could not point it out unless he had already heard it. At least, that seemed the most logical explanation.

Observing his perplexment, Caroline placed her hand on his forearm in a gesture of comfort as she explained, "If you had not been there to stop that Frenchman from stabbing Corporal Graham, we might have lost the entire war with Napoleon."

That seemed farfetched. And besides, it did not address the excruciating cause of his true grief. "But because of me, Charles is dead!"

"Charles was going to sign up whether you joined him or not. He was frustrated that more than a decade of war with Boney looked to be starting anew. He wanted no more wives of Chatternwell to be widowed. When Boney escaped, Charles informed you that he would fight with or without you because he was a good man. A courageous man."

William paused, thinking back on the events leading up to Hougoumont. Now that he thought about it, Charles had been the first to raise the subject of joining the fight after Boney escaped Elba.

"Charles would be proud of the part he played this day. That his loss prompted you to fly into a rage, which in turn led to saving the corporal. His presence here that day, it was—"

"A blessing?"

Caroline smiled. "Indeed. We did not need any more fatherless children in Chatternwell because of the little tyrant's quest for power. Charles had a choice in his fate because he was allowed to grow into a man. He had a mother and father who loved him, and he chose to honor them by protecting the liberty of England."

William sat down, his knees no longer able to hold him up as he adjusted his perspective of the past. He had lived in regret for five long years, but would he have done anything differently? Would he have convinced Charles to stay home, never himself signed up, based on what he knew now?

"Regretting the past is a waste of time, William. We must count the blessings and then continue with our lives."

Caroline had taken a seat beside him, her white skirts blinding in the sunlight as she placed her delicate hand over his. "Charles would want his sacrifice to be meaningful. He would want to know that his memory lived on through you. That you embraced life and lived it to its fullest as a mark of respect to honor his bravery and his sacrifice for the good of Chatternwell and other towns like it."

The chains that had bound him since this day at the fields of Waterloo slowly loosened their hold and the weight of them melted away. As the tight bands disappeared, William felt his eyes welling with moisture. Raising his hand, he found tears streaming down as he quietly came to terms with the past and released his guilt.

Next to him, Caroline resumed her melodic humming as he finally wept for his cousin's death, but accepted that it had played an important role within a hitherto unknown master plan.

* * *

WHEN WILLIAM'S eyes flickered open, he could feel his cheeks were wet. A surprising discovery, for he must have wept like a babe in his sleep. The room slowly came into focus as the dream faded.

He flinched in surprise when he realized Caroline was standing over him, with her hand on his arm as if to wake him up. She had lit a candle which was on the table beside her, her face lined with worry as she stroked him in a soothing gesture.

"William! Thank heavens you are awake! You were having a nightmare, and I could not rouse you."

He blinked to clear the haze of sleep from his eyes. "How did you know? What was I doing?"

"You were highly agitated, growling and flailing in your sleep, and then you … you were weeping?"

William swallowed hard and lifted himself to lean back against the arm of the settee. "I was counting my blessings."

"And that made you"—Caroline seemed reluctant to finish the question, clearly concerned for his pride—"cry?"

He thought about how to explain what had just happened. "I discovered that counting blessings can raise some deep emotions to the surface. I was grieving my past ... and releasing my failings. You were there."

She drew back in surprise. "In your nightmare?"

"It was a nightmare. One I have experienced frequently, but then you arrived and it ... changed to something else. Your words stayed with me, and I saw events from a fresh perspective."

"It was good that I was there, then?"

"Very good," he assured her.

Something within his soul had shifted, and for the first time in years, he felt a measure of peace. The dream version of Caroline had been right. Charles would not want to see him grieving still after so many years. This woman's words of wisdom before he had fallen asleep had provided the only comfort he experienced since his rage at Hougoumont, and now ... the entire future had taken on a new aspect.

Perhaps his vow to repress any emotion, to not form any relationships, to work to the exclusion of all else ... Perhaps it was a flawed commitment, and he needed to send the past to where it belonged—the past.

Which brought to mind the enticing presence of the woman who had helped lead him to this revelation. William's gaze dropped as he took in that Caroline's wrap had fallen open to reveal her night rail beneath, before rising to settle on her exquisite lips, and he imagined she might taste of the tea and biscuits they had eaten earlier that evening.

Once again, he wondered what her scent would be if he were to pull her down into his embrace.

* * *

CAROLINE WATCHED William's gaze focus on her lips, his tongue darting out to wet his own.

She recognized the heavy haze of desire that now played across his features, flushing his cheeks. Starting to back away, her blood heated feverishly in her veins as the blacksmith grinned to reveal a slash of white teeth. He certainly was more amiable than she had ever seen him, his grim air having dissipated to make him more approachable.

And, worse, even more appealing.

No men, Caroline! No men!

But she found herself utterly captivated by the heat blazing in his eyes. The desire to join the large, muscular blacksmith, to feel his hard body beneath hers, was intoxicating.

The air flickered with electricity, similar to working with woolen garments. She continued to shift back, but in her fascination, she had taken too long.

A powerful hand reached out to gently take her by the wrist, and he pulled her inexorably until she fell against him to watch in raptures as he raised his head toward her own.

* * *

WILLIAM LEANED UP, his lips meeting hers, and fire was born. Passion, as hot as the coals of his forge, erupted as he tasted her soft mouth. Caroline released a gratifying moan, her reciprocation of his desire clear. His tongue found its way into her mouth to confirm she tasted of tea. And woman. Sweet, soft woman.

William's fingers found their way to wind through her hair, relishing the silky length. Bringing the plait up, he breathed in deeply to find that she smelled of vanilla and peppermint.

My God! She is not just the embodiment of sunshine; she is Christmas itself!

She was in his arms. He had never beheld such a magnificent female, and now she was in his arms, moaning with her obvious desire for him.

Through the thin linen of his shirt, he could feel her unbound breasts pressed against his ribs. His lust mounted as his hands explored the shape of her delicate head, running over her cheeks and down her throat as their tongues licked and tangled as if they were starving for each other.

Caroline's delicate fingers combed through his hair, setting off streaks of pleasure that arrowed down to gather in his groin. William groaned, ever more hungry for her with every passing second. She was gorgeous, and soft, and responsive. And it had been so long since he had allowed himself any feeling or pleasure of any sort.

This incredible woman had unlocked him from the cell of his regrets, and he was utterly fascinated. He wanted to kiss her. Lick every inch of her body. Get inside her to sip on her very essence of sunshine and optimism.

He ran his large hands over her slight back to reach down and cup her buttocks and squeeze. Then he pulled on her rail to raise the hem.

Caroline moaned and gyrated against him. Once her rail bunched at her upper thighs, she parted her legs to straddle him. William's head fell back in ecstasy as her sweet, womanly mound made contact with his hardened length. He growled his approval as she squirmed against him.

* * *

IN A DAZE, Caroline realized William was no longer kissing her. His head was rolled back on the settee arm as he panted for air, holding her head tenderly to him with a large hand that covered most of her skull. He was so powerful; she felt like a delicate fawn in his arms.

Listening to the thudding of his heart in his chest, she was amazed at what had just happened. She had never felt such intense excitement, scarcely able to grasp that he had stopped.

Was he regretting their passionate embrace? Or was he attempting to be a gentleman by halting his passionate assault to the wall of chastity she had built around herself?

Caroline did not know what to think. Her test of her resilience had not proven her moral fortitude had improved these past years, but she could not bring herself to regret these past few moments in William's arms.

She knew the regret would come, but right now, she wanted to enjoy being embraced by a virile man whom she admired and liked.

There would be time to regret this in the morning, or the next, but for now she listened to the crackle of the fire and William's heart beating wildly with passion for her. It was the closest thing to contentment that she had ever experienced.

As they caught their breath, Caroline realized it was time for her to rise and move away from the blacksmith. How had such a fine specimen of manhood remained single? Why was he not married to an attractive young woman with several children already? She guessed he was a few years older than herself; old enough to be settled and young enough to enjoy it.

If William was married, you would not be lying in his arms on Christmas Eve.

She shut her eyes in painful regret. That might not be true, given her past mistakes.

With that reminder, the past came rushing back and Caroline recalled why she must stay away from virile men. She was not to be trusted. She did not trust herself.

Caroline pushed against him and made to rise, breaking their embrace. William allowed her, a fact which she did not know how to react to. Was she pleased or disappointed?

Bloody hell, this was why she stayed away from men. Because she turned into a dithering twit, as Lord Saunton had proved, and did stupid things because she received a tidbit of male attentions.

Caroline managed to get to her feet and walked away to stand in front of the fire. There she stood, staring into the glow as if she would find answers to her character flaws somewhere in the faint light.

Finding her voice, she finally spoke. "Would you like some tea?"

Truly? That is the first thing you could find to say?

Caroline squared her shoulders. She should be proud of what she had said. Her voice had been confident, giving no sign of her inner disturbance. It was best to act like nothing had happened and just attend to the man as the doctor had requested.

What was it about the holiday season that brought such vulnerable, private thoughts to the surface? If only it were a normal day and she could work on her walking dress. And if it were a normal day, the doctor would have found someone else to attend William Jackson and she would not now be confronted with the knowledge that her character was just as flawed as it had been two years ago. She had not matured at all. No, she had just discovered that she was still a flighty girl who could not be trusted around men, which was why she stayed far away from personal relationships.

No men, no opportunities to betray my friends.

No friends, no opportunities to betray them and lose their regard.

Work was the answer to her flaws. It kept her from making horrible mistakes and costing her beloved friendships.

William's voice was hoarse when he finally responded, "That would be appreciated."

Caroline gave a nod and left the room to make a pot of tea.

* * *

WILLIAM HAD KISSED THE MODISTE. Yet, he could not find it in him to regret it. She had resuscitated his dead heart and made it beat again. It was as if he had been deceased for five years and suddenly awakened to find an entire world of possibilities.

He was grateful she had moved away and offered the tea because the truth was, he was currently overcome. After detaching from his emotions for so long, he did not know what to do with the powerful feelings rushing up. He needed to accustom himself to this altered perspective.

What a revelation to discover that he had been punishing himself needlessly. He agreed with dream Caroline—he would best honor Charles's memory by respecting his sacrifice and building a future while his cousin remained in his memories.

But what did that mean?

Where do I go from here?

William had broken off the kiss, realizing he did not know what path he was careening down. His body had screamed at the interruption, determined to lay with the fine woman who had shown him a different way to think. Who had shared her optimism and did not know the repercussions of her advice.

He needed to find his footing. The future must be considered, and he would need a little time to adjust to the revelations of his dream and work through his thoughts. He did not know what he desired now.

But holding Caroline in his arms had been an unadulterated delight. He would gladly have continued, but that was not fair to her when he had no plans to pursue a courtship, or any relationships. After losing Charles as he had done, forming close connections was a mistake. He had just been handed the keys to the gaol, and he was hardly going to walk out, then walk right into another one. After five long years, he had just found his freedom, and he was going to take full advantage of it.

He should work out what he wanted, and he could not involve another person in the melee of his life as he opened his mind to reevaluate how he had been living. Yet he owed his newfound potential to her. Caroline had unlocked the despair in which he had been buried and shown him there were alternative paths to follow.

But what paths?

His business was a success, mostly due to his single-minded commitment to his work. He was at a point in his life where he could still reshape it. Income and work were not hindrances, so he just needed to decide what he wanted to do with this uncovered potential for happiness.

Blast, how did I reach this crossroad so swiftly?

Mere hours ago, he had clung to his state of numbness, shouldering the burden of guilt that beat him into a condition of unfeeling survival. Apparently, changing one's mind could be accomplished in an instant. Or in a recurring nightmare with a fresh infusion of perspective.

The only question that remained was ... *What do I want?*

69

He was a man with no ties or commitments outside of his work and sending money to his uncle and aunt, so he had the means to follow almost any future he desired. He could travel, perhaps visit the fields of Waterloo to pay his respects to his cousin. Or visit Italy and take in the sights of Ancient Rome. He could even move to the Americas if he wished.

The future might be an unanswered question, but he was grateful to the young woman for showing him he could accept his past without dishonoring Charles. She had no inkling the effect that she had had with her advice to count his blessings.

CHAPTER FIVE: THE PRESENT

*C*aroline was humming her carol in the kitchen. William was pleased to hear evidence that she had returned to her good spirits as she boiled water and moved around the back room.

Soon she returned with a tea tray, which included the rolled wafers she had given him earlier. He sat up slightly so he might drink his tea, while Caroline took a seat on the table before exploring his leg with gentle fingertips.

"The swelling appears reduced," she finally declared before standing to go take her seat on the other settee with her cup and saucer.

William shifted uncomfortably, putting his tea down while he tried to think about what to do.

Caroline evidently noted the movement of his hips. Putting her cup down firmly, she rose and walked across the room without a word. William twisted his lips, then brightened when he heard the creaking of the stairs as Caroline climbed them with soft thuds. She must have concluded what his needs were.

Shortly she returned downstairs, walking over to place a

chamber pot on the sitting room floor before leaving and closing the door behind her. William sighed his relief that he would shortly alleviate the pressure. As soon as he calculated how to do so without hurting himself.

With some careful exertions, he was eventually positioned back on the settee. "You can return!" he called out so she could hear in the other room.

The door opened, and Caroline came in holding a bowl of water and some cloths. She brought them over to place on the table, moistened a cloth, and handed it to him. William took it and discovered she had heated water to assist him in washing up. He smiled his gratitude as he used the cloth to wash his hands. He put it down on the tea tray, and she handed him another, which he used to mop his face and neck before placing it with the other soiled cloth.

"Thank you."

"Not at all. I should have thought of it before. You have been trapped here for hours."

She returned to her seat to drink her tea while William chewed on the wafers. They sat in amiable silence for a while until William finally broke the lull with a question that he had wondered about since their first meeting.

"Why did you move to Chatternwell, Caroline?"

Her brow furrowed slightly. "What do you mean? I came here to start my business."

"Yes, but … why Chatternwell? How did you choose this town? Are you from Wiltshire?"

Caroline colored slightly, stirring William's curiosity. Was the modiste embarrassed about something?

"I am originally from Somerset. My man of business searched for a good location to open a fashionable shop, but I wished for it to be in a smaller town with a strong community. Mr. Johnson did excellent research and found this location while I apprenticed with Signora Ricci in London on managing a millinery and dress-rooms of quality."

"You did not want to have your business located in London? Similar to … Signora Ricci?"

She shook her head. "No, I have no family left, and I miss the time I worked at Baydon Hall. There was a strong sense of community amongst the servants, and I enjoyed the support we provided each other. Chatternwell is a good town. The people are productive, the town is doing well, and one can build professional relationships with honest proprietors. London is too large and aloof for the likes of me. I … like it here. It feels more like a home."

William leaned back on the settee to stare at the beams of the ceiling while he thought about what she had revealed.

He had grown up here in Chatternwell. Worked here as a boy, and then a man. Other than leaving to fight Boney, he had been nowhere else. He had no other towns to compare it to other than the nearby town of Bath.

It was intriguing to hear his home described by an outsider who was here, not from the happenstance of birth, but by election based on a thoughtful evaluation. It made him appreciate, as he drifted back to sleep, what he had never taken time to consider. Caroline's words made him realize that, for better or worse, Chatternwell was his home.

WILLIAM SAT *in the back of the local church, in the very last pew. It was nearest the door, so it would allow him to leave quickly after the service. In other words, he could reduce how many of his neighbors he would need to engage with. When they visited him in his smithy, he could feign politeness for the sake of business. But after a church service, people were more garrulous. Friendly. They invited him to their homes for Sunday dinners. If he left in haste,*

73

he would offend fewer of the townsfolk and be able to return to his smithy to work without interference.

Although this could have been any given Sunday, William realized in a vague sense that he was dreaming because his ankle was miraculously healed. The last thing he could recall was falling asleep in his front room, and the soft sound of Caroline breathing deeply as she slumbered.

He tilted his head in an attempt to hear the vicar's words. For some reason, they were garbled as if coming from a great distance, but he could just make out the word manger. This must be Christmas service! If he had not injured himself, he would have been here for service this very day.

The vicar droned on, William scarcely able to hear any of it from the back of the church. He stood dutifully and sang hymns, sitting back down but prepared to run for the door as soon as he possibly could. Glancing up at the windows high behind him, William noted that the sky was overcast and it was snowing lightly.

Rustling in the pews ahead of him brought his attention back to the altar. People dressed in their Sunday best were beginning to stand, chattering to each other. The service must be over! Springing to his feet, he made for the exit, jamming his hat on his head as he opened the door to stride out into the wintry landscape beyond.

"Mr. Jackson!"

The voice was directly behind him—he could not pretend he did not hear. He continued to walk on, but threw a glance over his shoulder. "Dr. Hadley, how are you this fine Christmas Day?"

The doctor nearly ran to keep pace with him as William's longer legs ate up the distance down the path to the roadway. "I am well, Mr. Jackson. It is good to see you in fine health, sir!"

William threw a smile at the older man. He did not wish to offend Dr. Hadley, who he had to admit was a good sort. The doctor had taken care of the town's people for decades, accepting trade when they had not the means to pay. William reached the road and *started toward Market Street, his boots crunching on freshly fallen snow as the doctor hurried to keep up with him.*

William would relent his pace, but if he did, then more of his neighbors would engage him in conversation, and he wanted to build the new lock he had been thinking of. If it worked, the device could make him a fortune. Perhaps allow him to sell the smithy and live on its proceeds.

Beside him, Dr. Hadley was huffing in his effort to keep up. "Mr. Jackson, I would be remiss if I did ... not invite you to our Christmas feast ... I promised Mrs. Hadley I would!"

William halted. They were some distance from the church, and most of the parish was still inside. "That is very kind of you, Dr. Hadley. Tell your wife thank you, and bid her all the best wishes for the holiday season." He knew the doctor was merely being polite by extending the invitation. They had no true bonds between them. William had cultivated no friendships since his return from the war. These people would barely notice if he left town.

Dr. Hadley's face fell, his hat tilting to one side in his dejection before he reached up to straighten it. "You will not attend?"

"I would love to taste Mrs. Hadley's Christmas pudding, but I am afraid I am otherwise committed. Please, enjoy your feast and do not concern yourself with me. You have other guests to attend, I am certain."

"Yes, but ..."

William gestured back to the churchyard before tilting his hat. "Your wife is looking for you. Season's greetings, doctor."

When Dr. Hadley turned to locate his wife, William took the opportunity to walk away and turn in to Market Street.

Soon he was in his smithy, wearing his leather apron and studying a page covered in pencil drawings. He needed to heat the coal in his forge, and he could begin his work on the lock. He could, of course, have worked on this any day, but he had planned to work during the solitude of the holidays to keep his mind busy.

Just as he placed the graphite pencil down on the counter, the sound of humming began in the distance. Slowly, the humming grew in volume, and William realized he was to receive a visitor at the moment that the smithy door clicked and swung open. He knew who it would be before she came into view but, nevertheless, he was startled by her entrance when she appeared.

Her hair was glowing, lit from behind by weak sunlight, and she wore the frivolous cloak with the fur-lined cuffs that fell to the floor. She looked like an angel sent from heaven to scold him for working on Christmas Day, but her expression was benign and she smiled gently when she caught sight of him.

> *'Fear not,' said he, for mighty dread*
> *had seized their troubled mind;*
> *'glad tidings of great joy I bring*
> *to you and all mankind.'*

It was eerie, her staring directly into his eyes as she sang the verse.

He stepped back, his eyes widening with irrational fear at what she was to show him this time. She walked in, shutting the door and approaching him at the counter. With hazel eyes twinkling, she gazed up at him and asked, "Why are you working on Christmas Day, William?"

"I ... that is ... there is no one for me to spend it with." As he said the words, he wondered if it was true in light of Caroline's appearance once more in his dreams. Revelations from the earlier nightmare had proved that his philosophy about tamping down his emotions had been an error. Was she to reveal another aspect of his life to question?

Caroline held out her hand. Once again, it was clean, delicate, and perfect. His own were covered in soot from writing near the forge, and he was certain he bore smudges on his cheeks and forehead, but there was no point in balking. He held out his dirty hand to clasp hers.

"Chatternwell is a good town filled with good people."

"Yes, I do not argue that point, but—"

"Close your eyes."

William obeyed, shutting his eyes with the knowledge that it was futile to fight whatever was to come. The quiet of the smithy disappeared into a melee of merriment, and he could hear Dr. Hadley. Opening his eyes, he found that he and Caroline now stood in a dining room observing a Christmas feast.

Dr. Hadley sat at the head of the table, with his sons and their wives. Mrs. Hadley sat to his left, instead of the customary distance at the foot of the table. She was dressed in a fine velvet gown, with a lacy fichu draping her décolletage and matching the mobcap tied to her blonde hair.

Through the door, William could see a second table in the hall where children sat eating their Christmas pie.

The tables were loaded with plates, serving dishes, and gleaming silver. Wine had been poured, and a large Christmas goose had been carved. Hadley's eldest son finished telling an anecdote, and both men and women burst into laughter.

Caroline squeezed his hand and nodded her head to Dr. Hadley and his wife. They had their heads bent together, and Caroline drew him forward so he could hear what they were saying.

"You invited the blacksmith, and he declined?"

"Yes, Martha. I practically chased him down the street to deliver the invitation."

Martha was a cheerful, buxom woman who took part in charitable works about town. Her blonde hair was now streaked with gray, but her blue eyes were still lively with humor and intelligence. She had been a friend of William's mother, who had died when he was a boy, and she had always made a point of seeking him out to ask after his well-being. Guilt at his lack of interest in the generous woman suddenly presented itself, to William's dismay.

"I worry over little William." William nearly snorted—he was twice the size of Mrs. Hadley. *"He has not been the same since he*

77

returned from the war. I fear his mother would be most disappointed in me for allowing such aloofness to develop in her sweet boy. It is high time he finds himself a wife. A friend. Anyone."

"I quite agree. But what am I to do? Every holiday I invite him to join us, and every holiday he declines."

Martha peered over her shoulder toward her grandchildren, who were eating the feast with gusto, smiles of joy on their little faces as they chattered together. "I just wish he could experience the joy of family. He was such a happy boy, before he left to fight Boney. He never smiles anymore. It quite distresses me to think of the change in him. William is a good man."

Dr. Hadley nodded. "That he is. He runs an honest business and has created work for our men and boys."

William turned away. Why was Caroline doing this? He had finally rediscovered his living essence, but now he was to be confronted with the consequences of his self-imposed isolation. He tried to pull his hand from her clasp, but she would not let him. She broke off from her low humming. "Close your eyes, William."

He did so emphatically, not wanting to hear the rest of the conversation, nor to ponder his inadequacies. Inadequacies such as, he was all alone today while Dr. Hadley enjoyed a feast with loved ones. The man was building a veritable legacy with the sheer number of family and the seasonal elation to be found in this home.

William thought they would return to the smithy, but the sound of festive merriment was replaced by a crackling fire blended with the distant sound of waves crashing on rocks. His eyes flew open to discover Uncle Albert and Aunt Gertrude sitting at their dining room table with a small feast on it. A third place had been set, but there was no evidence of a guest.

Just as before, Aunt Gertrude appeared sad. She had appeared sad since learning of the death of Charles, her only child. William had not seen her cheery in some years. "I had hoped that this year he would come. He is all we have left."

Uncle Albert exhaled deeply. "Perhaps it was a mistake to leave Chatternwell."

Aunt Gertrude nodded. "It was. William has not been the same since ..." She struggled to a halt. "We should have stayed for his sake. Do you think ... he knows we love him?"

"I do not know, dear. You told him he was invited, I presume?"

"Every holiday. I told him there is always a place laid for him, if he ever changes his mind and finds the time to join us. I ... I just want him to be happy again."

William was stricken. He did not mean to cause his only family more pain than he already had.

Once again, he felt his eyes moisten, admitting to himself that his conduct had been selfish. He had not stopped to think that his beloved aunt might need him, that he had a responsibility. His life had been spared, while Charles had sacrificed his. It was William's duty to be there for his relations, to bring them some peace and not to be a cause of concern.

It was hard to stomach that his uncle and aunt had retired to Cornwall three years earlier, and William had yet to visit them.

Turning to Caroline, he pulled her firmly around by the hand so she stood in front of him. "Why are you doing this?" he demanded.

"No man can live alone, William. You must cherish the support of your friends. You must cherish the family you have left. You must accept that they are there for you, and you are there for them. You deserve to be loved."

William shook his head. He had not meant to cause any pain. This dream had left him with more questions than answers.

HIS ANKLE WAS THROBBING when William woke up. To his surprise, the clock on the mantelpiece proclaimed it was only eleven o'clock. This was turning out to be a very strange evening.

Near him, Caroline gave a little snort in her sleep and then, slowly, her eyes opened. Noticing he was awake, she sat up, throwing her blanket aside to swing her feet down to the floor. "Are you in need of something? Tea? Privacy for ..." Caroline gestured to where the chamber pot rested under the settee.

"No, just your company."

Caroline used both hands to smooth her hair and then straighten her wrap. "Oh."

"I was thinking about what you said. How Chatternwell is a good town, filled with good people."

She nodded, reaching over to take up her neglected cup and sip on its cold contents. "It is."

"It made me realize I have not appreciated what I have the way I should."

The corner of Caroline's mouth quirked up in a crooked smile. "You failed to count your blessings?"

"I did. It must be hard for you."

She frowned in confusion. "What do you mean?"

"You said you have no family. I am afraid I have not appreciated that I do. I can't imagine being entirely alone, with not one relation left."

Caroline's eyes flittered away. "It ... is difficult," she finally admitted in a thick voice.

"You have no one?"

William felt a pang when he noticed that her eyes now glittered and suspected that he had drawn tears to her eyes. What a bleak holiday they were sharing.

"I had some friends ... but I made a horrible mistake and lost them. I have learned to be self-reliant."

"And count your blessings?"

She chuckled, and William observed a flash of her usual optimism return. "And count my blessings."

"What blessings do you count tonight, Caroline?"

She inhaled a deep breath and thought.

"I have my own shop. I live in a lovely town and work with wonderful women. I must be viewed favorably because the doctor entrusted you to my care. I was to spend Christmas alone, but instead I am spending it … with you."

"I am a blessing?"

She cocked her head to the side, regarding him with a serious expression. "You are a good man who climbs his neighbor's roof on Christmas Eve to undertake secret repairs at his own expense. You are not … not a blessing."

It was William's turn to chuckle. "Thank you."

"You seem more cheerful than before?"

"Before?"

"Forgive me. You appeared to be a rather grim man. Tonight you seem … different."

"I have had time to reflect this evening, and it has me aware that I may need to change my ways. My mood. It might be time for me to embrace life more fully than I have done."

"To build a better future?"

He bobbed his head. "The future is vast uncharted land, and it might be time to explore it with a mind to make some changes."

"I find when the present is difficult, planning for the future can assist one through trying times," agreed Caroline.

William turned his head and contemplated her across the table. She truly was an intelligent and remarkable woman. One had to wonder why such a fine young woman was all alone in the world. Caroline should be married to someone kind, and be increasing with child.

She deserved to have all that she desired. Her business, a

family to replace the one she had lost, and many wonderful friends.

Here she was, taking care of him on the eve of Christmas and risking her reputation in order to be kind. He had no intention of ever growing as close to someone as he had been to Charles, whose absence was still a physical ache. Otherwise, he would pursue this fine woman for himself.

William shook his head slightly. A woman like Caroline would mean falling in love, and he could not bear another loss, such as Charles. Nay, he would need to stay away from her once this holiday was over, but he appreciated that she had shown him the error of his ways.

He could build a better future, allow for closer connections than he had these last few years. Appreciate the community he lived in and allow some emotions back into his life. This evening had changed him for the better, and he looked forward to the days ahead, now that he had time to think about the revelations of the evening. It was high time he took some time to visit his uncle and aunt at their seaside cottage. As soon as his injury improved, he would do so.

Caroline shifted and sat on the table. She felt his leg with gentle fingers.

"I am going to apply a fresh poultice. Would you like anything?"

"Warm water and cloths? Perhaps you could collect my nightshirt?"

"You would like to wash up?"

He nodded. "I was working in this shirt all day."

Caroline made a sound of assent, taking up things from the table and leaving for the kitchen. Soon she returned with the bowl of warm water and cloths, laying them out on the table. Once she left the room, he pulled his shirt off and took up one of the cloths to bathe himself.

The fresh, clean water was refreshing, and he felt considerably more comfortable when she came back in with his nightshirt, careful to avert her eyes from his naked torso as she handed it over.

Quickly, she cleared the table once more, and he could hear her tidying up in the kitchen while he pulled his nightshirt on. Leaving his buckskins on, he straightened up the settee pillows to settle back into a reclining position. This brief interlude of domestic bliss was a pleasant change in routine, especially given the time of the year. He was fortunate the doctor had found such an excellent companion to nurse him back to health. Spending the night with the wrong person would have been torturous, and Caroline's presence had brought much-needed respite through his dreams. For the first time in years, he had slept without dreaming of war and bloodshed, a minor miracle in itself. All in all, this Christmas Eve had been something of a success despite the swollen, bruised appendage.

Caroline returned to apply a fresh poultice, quietly tying it to his leg with a bandage. Then she cleared the room, and once again could be heard moving around the kitchen.

William drifted off to sleep in the darkened room, his body fatigued as he gradually slipped back into another dream.

CHAPTER SIX: THE FUTURE

EARLY MORNING, CHRISTMAS DAY (THE FIRST DAY OF CHRISTMAS)

*T*he sky was overcast—brooding and grim. Market Street was covered in a fresh fall of snow. The world was silent, muffled by the clouds overhead and flakes blanketing the roadway. William looked about and realized it must still be Christmas Day, the shops sporting festive Christmas boughs in their darkened windows. Across the street was the empty post office, the interior dark and deserted. If that was the post office, he must be standing in front of Caroline's shop.

He turned to look, noting a fresh display of ribbons through the window, along with festive sprigs and boughs draping the windows and counters.

Why was he back on this day? Was there some new revelation to uncover?

Not knowing what came next, William walked toward his cottage. As he approached a cross street, Dr. Hadley appeared, walking from the direction of the church.

"Mr. Jackson! Season's greetings to you!" The doctor paused to meet him at the corner. William realized something was not right. Dr. Hadley's hair was whiter, showing almost no signs of his former dark hair. His thick mustache was also white, and he had far more lines on his face. He appeared to have aged several years.

William rubbed his face, confused by this turn of events. Was this a future Christmas?

"Same to you and Mrs. Hadley, doctor."

"Thank you, Mr. Jackson. I must be on my way, but I don't need to tell you! You have a full house waiting for you!"

The doctor was not going to invite him to his Christmas feast as he did each year? And what did he mean ... a full house? While William pondered their conversation, the doctor had walked off in the direction of his home. He shook his head, not sure what to make of this new situation.

Shrugging, he resumed his walk home, feeling rather bleak and lonely. It would be lovely if Caroline showed up to guide him somewhere, the world eerily quiet as the snow began to fall once more.

An eternity later—the walk seeming to take much longer than usual—he reached his front door, where he stood hesitantly. All was quiet, and he was reluctant to enter his empty home and spend Christmas alone yet again. He wanted to embrace life, reconnect with his neighbors and family. Perhaps even visit Caroline in her millinery and converse with her while she worked—not enter his cold, silent cottage.

From behind the front door, he heard humming with a surge of pleasure. She was coming! They would accompany each other, and she would reveal some new way to improve his lot. It was sweet delight to hear her melodic voice break into song.

> *'All glory be to God on high,*
> *and to the earth be peace;*
> *to those on whom his favor rests*
> *goodwill shall never cease.'*

The sound grew closer until, finally, the lock clicked, and his front door swung open.

"William, there you are! We have been waiting to serve dinner!"

He blinked. Was she not going to ask him some peculiarly discerning question as she had before?

Caroline reached out a hand, and he looked down. This time she wore gloves, as if she were cold. Shaking his head in confusion, he looked down at his own hand to discover that he, too, was wearing gloves. At least this time, he saw no evidence of his hand being soiled as in the earlier dreams. He reached out and clasped her hand with confidence as she smiled and drew him closer.

Then, to his surprise, she bobbed up on her toes to plant a kiss on his cheek. Granted, it landed low in his beard because of their disparity in height, but it was comforting, nevertheless.

Caroline turned and pulled him along to guide him inside, William shutting out the cold outside to discover that the cottage was warm with ambient heat. The fires must be lit.

As he looked about the sitting room, he was startled to see Uncle Albert sitting at a table beside a young boy with almost black hair. They were studying a diagram sketched with a graphite pencil, their heads bowed together. William noticed the room had been redecorated. Above the fireplace hung a painting of Chatternwell at dawn, painted from one of the rolling hills. In it he could see the church spire, and chimneys were puffing cheerful smoke. The rug had been replaced with one of oranges and purples to pick out the colors of the painting, along with the pillows on the settees. New drapes hung in the windows, and the walls were painted in claret.

"Charles, do you wish to greet your papa?" Caroline called across the room. William's head whipped in her direction to confirm she was addressing the boy directly.

Were they not spectators of this scene, then? Were they active participants?

Looking back at the table, he saw the young boy raise his head. Blazing blue eyes found him standing there, and the boy hopped down from his chair to race across the room and throw his little arms around William's thighs. "Papa! You are home!"

William blinked several times, finally raising a hand to the boy's shoulder to give him a hesitant pat. Uncle Albert approached with a broad grin. "William, I have been teaching your boy about locks. I showed him the one you invented."

Uncle Albert indicated the table with a wave of his hand.

William was speechless, only able to nod mutely as he took in his uncle's cheerful demeanor. He had not seen Uncle Albert this happy in years.

Caroline dropped to her haunches in front of the boy. "Are you ready for dinner, Charles? Or do you need to wash your hands?"

The boy, no more than seven years of age, grinned with an impish twinkle in his intense blue eyes. "I must wash up," he confessed, then ran through the door to the kitchen.

Caroline pulled William by the hand and followed the boy. Entering the back room, William found Aunt Gertrude holding a small girl on her hip, tendrils of graying hair having escaped the neat little bun at her nape. It amazed him to see his aunt with a huge smile as she used a cloth to wipe the child's fingers, which were red with the juice of cranberries. "Now, Margaret, look what a mess you have made!"

"Aunt Gertrude?"

His aunt turned to smile broadly in greeting. "William, you are home! Dinner is almost ready, lad."

William had not seen his aunt in such fine spirits for years, not since he had broken the bad news about her son. Yet, here she stood with color in her cheeks and her eyes glistening with joy. His chest expanded with elation at seeing her in such good spirits.

The little girl in his aunt's arms looked about with wide, inquisitive eyes. Noticing William, her cherubic face lit up. "Pup-pa!" she squealed, wiggling with excitement to ignite a yearning.

He swallowed hard, looking carefully at the two children. Noting the boy bore a resemblance to himself, while the tiny girl wrapped in Aunt Gertrude's arm had blonde hair and lively hazel eyes. This was Caroline's daughter. His daughter?

On the table was the evidence of a dinner in its finishing stages, and the smell of roasted meat caused a rumble in his belly. The entire room was filled with domestic bliss and festive spirits, sprigs of holly adorning the windows, and William felt true happiness standing in his kitchen surrounded by the ones he loved.

Turning to Caroline, pulling on her hand to get her attention, he questioned her earnestly. "What is this?"

She gazed at him with hazel eyes before responding, "This is the future, William. If you allow it."

William was overcome, his throat growing thick with the sheer emotion enveloping him as he took in the sight of his uncle and aunt restored to good spirits. New life that had been brought into the world and set things right, with two healthy children to build the future.

Turning, he pulled Caroline into an embrace. He wanted this! All of this. He wanted children, and hope. He wanted reconciliation and good cheer. He wanted her!

As he engulfed her with his arms, feeling her slight body against his own, she giggled. "Careful, William. Do not squish our babe." Which was when he felt the roundness of her belly pressed against him. Caroline was increasing, and with this news he nearly wept his joy into her vanilla-scented hair.

"Merry Christmas, sunshine," he whispered into her hair, feeling her lips curve into a smile against his neck.

"Merry Christmas, blacksmith."

* * *

SHE WAS HALF ASLEEP, dozing on the shorter settee and wishing she could stretch out properly on a bed, when Caroline heard the blacksmith mumbling in his sleep.

She could not make out the rest of the words, but she could pick out one.

"… sunshine …"

What on earth could the blacksmith be dreaming about?

She dug an elbow into the settee cushion and raised her head to peer across to where he lay.

"… Christmas …"

Caroline tried to see his expression in the darkened room. Was he in distress? Should she waken him once more?

"… Caroline …"

She bit her lip. He was dreaming of her!

One of Chatternwell's most eligible men was currently prone across the room and dreaming of silly little Caroline of Somerset. An orphan and unchaste woman of few redeeming traits!

What a bizarre situation this was proving to be. There was nothing to compare this night to, no similar experience to call on. She did not know what to make of the strange events that had unfolded these past hours.

In a day or so, she would leave this cottage and return to the real world, outside of this strange interlude. When she and William met in the future, they would have to pretend this had never happened. In fact, they would have to return to their aloof relationship as Mrs. Brown and Mr. Jackson, their only commonality being that they each owned a business on Market Street. This entire evening would be washed away as if it had never happened.

This realization was unexpectedly … desolate. She liked the blacksmith, especially since he had relaxed his grim mood and revealed some of his struggles.

Many women in this town coveted William for his handsome form and successful livelihood. Yet Caroline knew something else about him. She was the only woman in Chatternwell aware he had injured himself while secretly helping the old widow next door by repairing her roof on Christmas Eve.

He was an honorable man, and she had to admit their earlier conversation was thrilling, when he had confessed that she had influenced his thoughts and lightened some undisclosed burden he had been carrying. The shift in his mood was palpable, and she was apparently the cause of it.

The thought of gathering her things to walk out the door was rather disheartening.

Work!

Caroline drew a deep breath, slightly mollified at the reminder of what would take the place of this increasingly intimate connection she was forming with William.

Work will keep your mind from wandering about!

She nodded to herself. Close relationships were not permitted. This was an aberration, a freak occurrence. Once this holiday was over, so too would be this strange bond they had formed over the course of the night. Work would distract her from any yearnings that might disturb her thoughts.

As she reached this conclusion, feeling better for having a plan to get past these unprecedented events, Caroline realized that William's eyes were open. He was staring at her with the oddest expression. Was it ... admiration?

Caroline sat up. "Do you need anything, William?"

He licked his lips to moisten them, then spoke in a low voice. "Would you check my ankle?"

"Of course!" She swung her feet to the floor and bounced up, quickly navigating the room to light a candle before sitting on the low table. She pulled his blanket up to reveal his ankle in the low light, then gently felt around.

"It seems considerably less swollen. Shall I replace the poultice?"

William shook his head, reaching out a hand to take hold

of the edge of her wrap. Caroline's mouth went dry as her gaze dropped to his powerful, bronzed hand. She noticed with fascination the dusting of black hair on the back of his hand as awareness arrowed to her loins to thicken and pool.

"You are an extraordinary young woman, Caroline Brown." His voice was husky, his eyes emanating heat to reflect the coiling in her lower belly.

"I … am?" she croaked out before swallowing hard, tension thrumming between them, their gazes locked.

"And very beautiful. The most beautiful woman I have ever beheld."

Caroline swallowed hard again. "That is not possible. What of Miss Jolie, the daughter of Sir Walter?"

His lips quirked in amusement. "I am not well acquainted with Miss Jolie, but she has never turned my head. You, on the other hand, have refused to leave my head since we met."

At this revelation, Caroline blinked. "You have been thinking … about me?"

"Aye" was his only response as he continued to finger the wrap between his thumb and forefinger. Desire coursed through her veins. Caroline was tempted to fall forward, only holding herself back by sheer force of will as she focused on his lips and relived their kiss from earlier that night. Her skin still tingled from the scrape of his beard.

William drew a deep breath, and then reluctantly released the fabric to drop his hand to the settee. "If you wish to remain a maiden, you shall have to walk away now, sunshine."

Crushing disappointment overcame her. Her lips formed words without thought. "I am … not … a maiden."

Her shameful whisper was as loud as a shout, with no nocturnal sounds other than the crackling fire to disguise her words. Caroline clapped a hand over her mouth in dismay.

Why would you tell him that?

William stared at her, then slowly frowned in the dim flicker of the candlelight. "You are widowed? I thought Mrs. Brown was an honorific. How did you not inform me of this before now?"

Caroline flushed. The heat raced across her skin, and she feared her mortification would singe the roots of her hair.

"Nay … I am …" Her courage failed. For several thick seconds, she could not speak past the lump in her throat. "I am not extraordinary, William. I … I am a fallen woman!" she proclaimed shrilly into the darkness, barely able to breathe as she realized she had admitted the truth out loud.

Clapping a hand over her mouth once more, distressed that she had done it. Destroyed their burgeoning affection. She had wanted to prolong their shared intimacy, but her impulsive words had driven a permanent wedge between them. There had been a wish to share herself, but now her thoughtless declaration would cause him to lose his regard and she would return to her isolation. If she was fortunate, he would keep her secret.

Caroline squeezed her eyes shut in regret. It had been so long since she had let her walls down to share a genuine experience with another person. There were so many excuses she could state for having done so now. It was the holidays. She was lonely. William was the first man to gaze at her with such blazing admiration.

None of it signified because she had revealed her darkest secret to a veritable stranger and now he would display his disdain and she would be alone once more.

Her throat tightened, and threatening tears burned.

Eventually, she realized she could no longer avoid his reaction and her eyes flickered open. The blacksmith was watching her, contemplating her declaration. Caroline wished she could sink into the table and disappear until, what seemed an eternity later, he finally responded, "I have done too much bad in my life to judge you."

His reply loosened the bands of despair wrapped around her chest as she finally sucked air into her burning lungs.

* * *

WILLIAM HAD every intention of wooing the incredible woman who sat by his side. After the potential future his dream had revealed, her fate was sealed. He was going to marry Caroline Brown and live in sunshine for the rest of his days.

However, he realized, she had not shared the experiences of his dream, so his decision would appear abrupt. He had yet to convince her they were fated to be together.

Sensing there was more to her declaration regarding her shame, William concluded he did not care what dark past she might be hiding. Whatever had prompted her to move to Chatternwell was irrelevant to his determination to entwine his future with hers.

William had seen into her heart, and the beauty of her spirit utterly beguiled him. She had brought him back from the dead with her talk of blessings, and the value of friends and family, and finally with her views on the future.

There was no possibility, now that the light had cast away the shadows of his past, that he would relinquish her.

All that remained was to lead her to a similar conclusion. That life would be meaningless without him at her side.

Then the vicar would read their vows, and Caroline would come to live in his home. She would change his life as she saw fit, and he would worship her from this day forward while they shared the joy of creating their own family together.

Somehow, he had to bring her to this decision with determined subtlety.

Since he had opened his eyes, he had been aware of her. Enthralled by her presence, he was compelled to draw her closer to within his reach.

Now that he knew she was not a maiden, thick desire coiled through his body and all he could think of was the need to pull her gently over to lay her soft body over him. Lush curves visible through the thin fabric of her wrap and night rail made his mouth water, and he could almost taste the sweetness of her fair skin.

William licked his dry lips and considered his next move before noting that Caroline's gaze was fastened to his. She was flushed, and her breathing quickened. Perhaps she was as fascinated as he?

He drew a breath and took a chance, raising his hand to reach for her tentatively. Triumph swelled his lungs when Caroline came willingly into his arms. Her hazel eyes were dark with liquid desire and, when her lips parted with a sigh, it was the only invitation he needed.

William wrapped an arm around her slight waist to embrace her close before sliding his hands up to cup her chin, tilting her head back for a searing kiss, his mouth claiming hers as if he were starving. Her fingers dug into the thick muscles of his arms as she kissed him back, her lips parting as he licked at her plump lower lip. Without hesitation, he swept his tongue to devour her mouth. Their tongues danced together as Caroline returned every swipe, every caress, with a passion to match his own.

He felt her gentle fingers exploring the firm contours of his torso as she moaned, her hips jerking against his to send shooting pleasure into his loins as his craving mounted. Blood pounded in his ears with a deafening roar while her soft sighs drove him wild. Groaning loudly, he took her face between his palms to end their kiss and to stare into her lovely hazel eyes. She frowned with uncertainty until her eyes followed his fingers as they slid down to work the knot of her wrap. Wriggling, she helped him to divest her of the garment, which he pushed off her shoulders, and then they struggled together to get it off her arms, the sleeves folding back clumsily in their haste.

Her hips jerked into him as she raised her upper body to assist him, the sensation of her mound thrusting against him causing his length to harden in excitement. Eventually they had the garment off, and he tossed it to the other settee before pulling her head down with a determined hand to kiss her once more. His hands swept down her back to cup her rounded buttocks firmly, and he nudged his engorged length against the seam of her sex, quickly growing frustrated at the layers between them.

William's hands sought the hem of her rail, pulling roughly at the edge to lift it until it got stuck, trapped between their upper thighs. Caroline moaned in frustration before pressing her hands into the settee, bracketing him as she lifted her hips. William panted, breathing in her scent of peppermint and vanilla as he swept the rail up to bunch under her arms. He had not allowed his gaze to venture down to her nakedness, instead focusing on divesting her of the garment.

Caroline's knees came down on either side of his hips, and she rose back to fight with the rail and throw it aside. And William stopped breathing as he finally beheld her magnificent body.

She had lovely, rounded breasts with straining pink tips. His mouth watered in anticipation while he caressed over the pebbled nipples with his ardent gaze before slowly taking in the expanse of her smooth belly. Then he blinked hard, shutting his lids with sheer lust at the sight of the blonde curls that shielded the shadowed apex between her legs.

* * *

CAROLINE hardly comprehended how things had developed to where she was now naked and seated around, over, on the powerful physique of the blacksmith. Her thoughts were incoherent. She vaguely recollected the admiration she had seen in his eyes before they crashed together into increasingly ravenous kisses, their tongues and lips melding into one as if they could not get close enough. As if they were attempting to be one unit rather than two separate people.

She panted from the vigor of the past few minutes, attempting to collect herself, but she had never experienced such passion. The blacksmith was intoxicating in his masculinity. Intoxicating in the deep affection and regard she had seen in the depths of those dark blue eyes. It was the first time she had admitted even a small part of her secret shame, and William had heard what she had told him, considered her confession, and then acknowledged her without judgment. The sheer relief of letting her guard down only to find acceptance in response nearly burst her heart with incredible joy.

Her only experiences with passion had been furtive, guilt-stricken, and she could not pretend there had been any true connection with the man she had given up her integrity and self-worth for. Lord Saunton had been an accomplished lover, but they had shared no true sentiment, and their encounters had been hasty lest they be caught, which, eventually, they had been. The earl had changed considerably since the time they had met in the stables, but back then his charm had been fickle and his regard was only for her body.

There could be no comparing that time with the present.

Or William. This was a true man, worshiping her with his avid stare as she looked deep into his heated eyes. Over the past hours, they had developed a true rapport, and under other circumstances, she would be proud to call her fellow merchant a valued friend.

Caroline suspected that at some point she would deeply regret what was unfolding, but she could not think about what would happen when she returned to the reality of her life. In the present, she felt as powerful as Aphrodite to have enraptured a man such as William Jackson. The man was infamously disinterested in the women of Chatternwell since taking over the ownership of the smithy, but here he lay between her legs, captivated by her femininity.

She felt at once beautiful and compelling for the first time she could remember. Caroline wanted this moment, suspended out of time, to last forever. Reality would set in, along with the crushing guilt she bore for her past mistakes and the betrayal of her dearest friend, but right now she would grab hold of this respite. Treasure it long after this evening's strange events were a distant memory to hold close in the lonely hours when she did not work. True passion, a true meeting of the minds, had not seemed possible for her, but this aberrant night held precisely that.

Frantically, she pushed his nightshirt up to bare his torso. Reaching down with trembling fingers, she awkwardly unbuttoned the falls of the painfully tight buckskins. In his burning desire, William's impressive length was straining to be free. He hissed as her fingers grazed against his naval, but Caroline barely noticed, her folds swelling and pulsing in anticipation of what was to come.

Finally, she released him to discover he was as hard as iron, his swollen member jerking in the grasp of her soft palm. William growled, rolling his hips.

Caroline stared down at him, discovering how empowering this position was for her, towering over the large man and holding his length in her hand.

"I need to undress."

She chuckled at the low, reverberating declaration. Lowering her foot onto the floor, she hopped off of him. William quickly pulled off his nightshirt before lifting his hips to push down his buff-colored buckskins and small clothes, growling in frustration when they caught on his legs and attempting to sit up.

Caroline quickly leaned over and untied the leather tapes at his thick calves, then unbuttoned the leather-covered buttons that fastened the breeches to below his knees. Taking hold of the garments, she yanked them down over his bandaged ankle. She straightened them and turned to fold them over the table reverently. Buckskins were a financial investment, and she wanted to ensure they would be unharmed.

When she turned back, she found that William's entire naked body was revealed, except for the solitary stocking he had not removed from his uninjured leg, causing her lips to curl up in a half smile before she grew utterly distracted. In her prior trysts with the earl, she had not seen much in their hurried encounters. Caroline was at once curious and mildly shy to behold William in such an intimate state.

Good Lord, he was a powerfully built man. His shoulders would have been broad under any circumstances, but pounding iron and steel every day for years had hardened them into muscular planes only hinted at with clothing to shield them from sight. Dark, curling hair covered the expanse of his chest before arrowing down over a flat, sculpted stomach. His most impressive feature was the proud length standing to attention. Her knees weakened as she considered mounting the powerful appendage, her inner muscles thrumming in anticipatory delight at the idea of seating herself over him to ride him to mutual completion.

Their position on the settee should have been awkward. Ungainly. But now that William's powerful physical condition was revealed, she realized it was barely an effort for him to lift her slight form.

William's hot gaze traveled over her body, reminding her that she was as naked as he was. More naked than he, because she had no stocking on. There, with only the fire in the hearth and a single candle to light the darkened room, they gazed at each other with only the sound of their mutual panting and the crackle of flames on wood to break the silence between them. Caroline, in a haze, acknowledged it was the calm before the storm.

CHAPTER SEVEN: THE CRESCENDO

*C*aroline was the incarnation of everything he found desirable. Intelligent. Ambitious. Beautiful. She smelled sweet, and her responsive nature was a hitherto hidden delight. Every cell of his body craved to join with her softness.

As they stared at each other through the warm gloom, William finally lost his patience. He needed to feel her naked skin against his. He had imagined it a hundred times before and could wait no longer.

"Come back," he growled.

She hesitated for only a second before lowering her naked form over his. William gasped at the touch of her skin, blinking in an effort to maintain his focus as he grasped her waist to lift her upright. Craning up, he licked at one of her pink, pebbled nipples. She moaned and gyrated against him, shooting sensation straight through him to gather in his groin.

It seemed impossible, but his cock lengthened further as he suckled her hardened nipple. Caroline arched back, pushing more firmly against his mouth and crying out in shocked raptures. William chuckled before sweeping his mouth to her other breast to swirl the tip before gently grazing it with his teeth. She cried out again, keening as he swept his hands down over the flare of her hips. He continued to suckle on her sweet nipples until she was writhing in mindless pleasure, before using his hands to pull her down his body.

Caroline's thighs fell open in invitation, her knees sliding down over his outer thighs to meet the settee with a slight thud as her slick crease made contact with his erection. William groaned as he pressed himself up against her core, lightheaded with lust when she lifted her hips to slowly seat herself onto his hard, aching length, nearly spending when her wet heat encircled his cock in a tight embrace.

Both of them paused, trying to catch their breath while William found his bearings. Disbelief assailed him from the overwhelming sensation of being joined with Caroline. He looked up at her, lit by candlelight, and attempted to comprehend that this dazzling woman was somehow positioned to ride him on his settee. She was magnificent, all pale skin and soft curves rising above him like Venus from the ocean. Her blonde hair had come loose from her plait, and her expression was as shocked as he imagined he must appear to her.

He lifted a hand to brush back a strand of her flaxen hair, threading his fingers through the tangle of fronds to cup her head and stare deep into her eyes when, with a sudden gasp of pleasure, she bucked her hips. Her head fell back in sensuous abandon as she continued to rock over him, and his hands dropped to grip her by the thighs as she rode him.

William moved to stroke and circle the nub at the apex of her swollen crease, teasing moans from her throat as she rocked her hips. Caroline's eyes fell shut as she jerked in response, moving rhythmically in time to his forefinger as he gently explored and flicked, finding the precise location that made her keen the loudest. Once he found her preference, he worked her relentlessly, watching her desire mount with fascination until he felt her peak, her intimate muscles pulsing around his hardened length.

As he felt her slow in the aftermath, he thrust up deep, growling as all the pent-up pressure in his soul unraveled. Frantically, he increased the tempo of his thrusts, using his hands to grasp her hips and move her faster as she gyrated and rode him to his own peak. Without warning, William lifted her by the hips, spending in a silvery stream over his own torso while the white-hot sensation of his climax made him lose all sense of self.

* * *

SEVERAL MINUTES PASSED as she fought to recover her breath, seated on his thick thighs while she slowly descended from the heights of shared passion. Eventually, she rose to clean up and put her night rail back on. Embarrassment was setting in.

What have I done?

She had lain with a man who was not her husband. Again. A hand came up to rub the ache in her chest.

This served to prove she was a harlot. An unchaste woman.

She handed William a rag to clean himself, unable to meet his eyes, before walking over to the other settee to pick up her wrap. As she lifted the garment, she heard William settle back behind her.

"Join me?"

Caroline stared down at the embroidered fabric in her hand, uncertain how to respond and attempting to make sense of his request.

"Please?"

Tears sprung into her eyes. This was unprecedented. Did the blacksmith want to … cuddle? With her? She glanced over to him. His blue eyes were intense, even in the low light of the dim room, and as before she saw admiration, perhaps even affection, in his gaze.

Without quite making the decision, she moved closer. William shifted over to create some space, holding up an arm in invitation. Caroline did not know what to make of it, but the urge to settle next to him could not be denied. She lay down beside him, wrapping a slender arm around his large body.

The blacksmith tucked her head under his chin, his muscled arm holding her close in an embrace. After a few minutes, it became clear he had fallen asleep, his breathing even. Caroline listened to his heart thudding in his chest, the heat of his body seeping into hers. She could not deny her amazement. William seemed to hold her in genuine regard. Shame slowly dissipated.

She had briefly broken her vow not to grow close to anyone. Caroline knew from past mistakes that she could not be trusted to uphold her loyalty to her friends, but just for tonight, she would enjoy the brief respite from her exile from good company. Beyond comprehension, the blacksmith seemed to like her, and she was going to grab hold of this moment and clutch it as long as she could before she had to walk away tomorrow and return to her solitude.

Once more, she had proven that she was weak, but just for the one holiday, she wanted to forget her failings and accept William's attentions until reality inevitably imposed itself. The feel of his heartbeat against her cheek was soothing, and soon she drifted off.

When she awakened, the room was lit with the gloom of a winter morning. The neglected candle had burned out, and the fire was low. She lifted her head from the blacksmith, making to rise, but he growled in his sleep and pulled her close, causing Caroline to blink rapidly in confusion. Was this what it was like to be married to a kind man who loved his wife?

Work, Caroline! Do not get any ideas about love and companionship!

She lay there, scarcely breathing. The notion was so tempting. The reminder of work, which usually worked so well to settle her mind, did not currently hold any appeal. She wanted to stay in his warm embrace and listen to him breathing.

William smelled of leather, and fire, and soap, and vaguely metallic. She snuggled closer and fell asleep, feeling safe in the cradle of his arm.

When she awoke once more, she found William was kissing the crown of her head. She looked up into his eyes, fascinated by the blue depths. He smiled, creasing the corners of his eyes before gently kissing her forehead.

"I am afraid I need privacy," he whispered.

Caroline immediately lifted her head. He slowly relinquished his hold, and she rose to her feet. "Do you need any help?"

"A fresh poultice and water to clean up would be appreciated."

She nodded, clearing the table of its remnants and heading out the door, which she closed behind her so he might use the chamber pot in peace. Looking about the kitchen, she put water on to boil. Soon she had washed the cloths from the night before and prepared tea and sandwiches, along with a fresh poultice.

Calling out to confirm William was ready for her entrance, she opened the door and brought in a tray to place it down on the table.

William smiled at her, thanking her for the supplies. He straightened up, shifting into a seated position. He wore only the long nightshirt, his buckskins neatly folded on the table, and he had fresh stubble showing higher on his cheeks where he shaved the shape of his beard. Caroline thought he looked wonderful, and she could not help imagining that they were married as they shared the domestic bliss of breaking their fast to sip on their tea.

Once she had finished her sandwich, she settled back. "I shall clean up and then I must attend Christmas service. My absence would raise questions."

"As will mine," he replied gruffly.

"Yes, but eventually the town will know you were injured. My absence will not have a convincing explanation."

William tilted his disheveled head in assent. "You should go."

"I do not know how long it will last, but after I shall pick up my order from Mr. Andrews and then return to feed you."

"Thank you. For everything you have done."

Caroline smiled, blushing a little with pleased unease. "I am reluctant to leave. It is as if I have been dreaming, and now I must wake to find that the world is the same as it was yesterday."

William regarded her before finally responding in a husky tone, "It was no dream. Everything has changed."

Her brow creased slightly at this statement. The blacksmith must realize that this interlude must end. As much as she wanted to prolong their strange kinship, eventually life would intrude. She had nothing to offer a man like him. Despite his acceptance of the inadequacies she had voiced the night before, William did not know how deep her perfidy ran. She could never reveal the depth of her betrayal to Miss Annabel. Even as understanding as he had been, there would be no possibility of retaining his affection if he learned what she had done to her closest friend.

Uncomfortably, she cleared her throat and stood. "I shall clean up before I leave for service."

* * *

WILLIAM LAY BACK, a book on his breastbone, but his gaze fixed on the beams of his ceiling. Once Caroline had left via the back door, an eerie silence had fallen over his cottage. He felt he was in one of last night's dreams once more, the crackling of the fire the only evidence he was, indeed, awake.

He regretted the sequence of events. Caroline was to be his wife, but his desire for her had overtaken him in the early hours and it was unclear where they stood.

Courting her properly would have been a better strategy, but he had been caught up in the magic of their connection and lost his senses. Hopefully, this would not impede his intended courtship.

It nagged at him that Caroline was hiding something. Something she was ashamed of. It was clear she did not realize that there was nothing she could reveal that would change his mind about his intentions. While she had been here, in his home, he had been entirely confident that the future he had foreseen would materialize. Now that he was alone, he was nervous that obstacles would arise.

He must convince Caroline they were meant to be together before she left this evening to return to her work. Their connection seemed inextricably entwined with the magic of the holidays, and he was worried that if they parted without an understanding, it would be difficult to rediscover this wonderful enchantment they had shared.

William could only hope that the vicar did not get carried away and keep the community in service for hours. It was hard to predict what the clergyman would do, and William needed all the time he could get to woo Caroline into an understanding before their day ended.

* * *

CAROLINE SHIFTED on her rented pew; one of the privileges of her increased income was that she no longer had to stand in church for the entire service.

The vicar delivered a lengthy sermon from his pulpit, but she barely heard a word of it. Could there be a worse place to visit in the aftermath of her repeated failings than this, the holiest of places?

She could only be grateful that it was a Christmas service of good tidings, rather than a sermon on the evils of man.

Rising to sing a hymn, her eyes fixed on the book in her hand, Caroline tried to make sense of her decisions. Her lips formed the words of the lyrics as her thoughts continued to race.

This connection with William differed from what she had experienced with the earl. Logically, she was aware of that, but it did not change the fact that two years earlier she had betrayed her friend in the most horrible manner that a woman could betray a friend.

It was ill-advised to lie with a man outside of wedlock. The possibility of children was an ever-present concern. Annie Greer had had a hard life with only one parent to take care of her financially, but at least she was in a reputable situation and did not have to contend with the additional burden of bastardy.

As the hymn ended, and the congregation once more took their seats, except for the poorer townsfolk who stood together in the section without pews, Caroline's eyes fixed on the stained-glass windows.

It was ill-advised to lie with a man, but that was not the crux of her vow to remain aloof from others.

If she were honest with herself, the loss of the connection to Baydon Hall, to Annabel and Mrs. Harris, along with many of the other servants, had been devastating to a girl who had no one left in the world. They had been her only family until she had betrayed them so horrifically.

That Miss Annabel had seen fit to give her a reference and find her a new position had only emphasized what Caroline had forfeited with her terrible decision to dally with Lord Saunton.

She could never survive losing all her connections again. First, she had lost her parents as a young girl. Then her grandmother and only remaining relation. Later, as an adult, she had thrown away her acquired family in exchange for the glib attentions from a handsome nobleman. Losing everyone she loved for a fourth time was not to be borne. If she could not trust herself to remain loyal, she could not allow herself to form any close relationships.

Unfortunately, now that she was no longer in the presence of the blacksmith, Caroline was very much afraid she had grown far too close to William already.

She wished she was with him now, sharing a Christmas feast.

What had happened to her vow to remain detached? To focus on work? It kept her life simple to fill her waking hours with the bustle of activity and allowed her to keep her vow without risk of entanglements.

As she stood once more, turning to the next hymn, Caroline put her musings firmly aside. This was a problem for tomorrow. For this afternoon, she would share a Christmas feast with the blacksmith and eke out every second of joy she could from spending the holiday with someone. Anyone. Especially such a compelling man who exhibited such affection. A man whose company she genuinely enjoyed. She might never have another opportunity to experience the pleasure of his company, so she was going to relish this last Christmas memory before she must endure the coming seasons of her life truly alone. The universe had favored her with one last holiday to cherish, and she only had a few hours remaining before she returned to her normal life.

The hymn ended and Caroline sat once more until she realized that the service must have ended. Men and women, dressed in their Sunday best, were standing in pews in discussion about their holiday plans. Caroline stood up to exit the pew. Annie skipped from the standing section to meet her in the aisle. "Merry Christmas, Mrs. Brown!"

Caroline smiled down at the girl, pleased to see the flush of rosy cheeks and the gloss of silky hair. Annie looked so much healthier than when they had met several weeks ago. "Merry Christmas, Annie!"

"Did you enjoy the service?"

Caroline sincerely could not say. The words of the vicar had been lost with such pressing concerns weighing on her. "I did. Are you going to pick up your goose from Mr. Andrews?"

"Yes, Mum and I will leave shortly." Annie turned to wave to her mum, who was in conversation with a fellow war widow. Mrs. Greer waved back, smiling broadly at Caroline and gesturing her thanks. Mrs. Greer had been gaunt when Caroline first met her several weeks ago, but now she had color in her cheeks and the glow of improving health. Caroline was pleased she had been able to help. Chatternwell had a number of war widows, which had strained the townspeople's resources. Taking responsibility for the Greers as a new business owner made her feel part of her new community.

Caroline finished talking with Annie and hurried ahead of the crowd to walk to the baker. Turning in to Market

Street, she strode swiftly to the shop, knocking on the door to get Mr. Andrews's attention. She must be the first person to arrive from the service. He came over to let her in, and Caroline collected her order, which she had paid for earlier in the week. With great relief, she hurried back to her shop so that if anyone was passing, they would see her entering the millinery before she exited from the back.

Making her way along the alleyway at the back, and noting the brooding winter sky, Caroline chuckled when a chilly wind worked its way up the exaggerated cuffs of her green velvet cloak.

The blacksmith was correct that it was a highly impractical garment for dissuading the cold, but she loved it because it was so pretty and feminine. An eccentric creation that simply made her happy to don.

Reaching a cross street, Caroline glanced around to ensure no one was about to see her approach the blacksmith's cottage. Once she confirmed the way was clear, she raced across the street to enter the alley on the other side. Excitement to see William again caused her pulse to race as she walked quickly, holding her skirts aloft to ease her passage.

WILLIAM'S SPIRITS lifted when he heard the back door swing open, and he struggled into a seated position. Caroline soon appeared, flushed with delightful color and her eyes blazing with excitement.

"I have returned!"

"I have waited with bated breath for your return."

She beamed at him, and William inhaled with exhilaration. It would seem he might succeed in his quest before she left at the end of the evening. Today he was going to court the magnificent modiste who had stolen his heart.

"I find it ridiculous that the man who repairs locks for a living has one that clearly needs replacement."

William laughed. "Alas, I have no time to repair my home. I am always occupied with work. However, a modiste should know how to fashion cloaks that would not lead to freezing in cold weather." He gestured at the cloak she still wore.

Caroline laughed in return. "I shall prepare our meal. How is your ankle?"

"The swelling is down considerably, and it does not hurt unless I move it too quickly. I think it might not be as badly sprained as it first appeared when the doctor was here. Or your poultices were especially effective."

She smiled again. "I am so glad. You will be able to return to work with little delay. It must bore you to lie about."

William beckoned her closer, taking up her delicate hand in his. Staring up into her eyes, he confessed in a husky voice, "Not when you are here."

She bit her lip before smiling. Caroline appeared pleased with the compliment. "I should make our meal."

He reluctantly released her hand, wishing he could follow her into the other room, but that would be against the doctor's orders. "Be quick," he implored.

She gave a nod before retreating to the back.

William lay down, whistling the tune of the carol that Caroline had sung in his dreams while he listened to her move about in the next room. Once they were married, she would always be within reach. They could share their evenings in front of the fire. Perhaps impart business advice about their respective merchant ventures. One day they would have children to share their evenings and holidays with, including adorable little girls with flaxen hair and enchanting hazel eyes.

Breathing deeply in contentment, he continued to whistle as he contemplated how much Caroline had changed his life in the space of an evening. It must be the magic of the season. Or the magic of her.

When she entered the room with a tray laden with food, he swung his legs down to the floor. "I feel ashamed to watch you toil while I lie about like a lazy oaf," he confessed.

She giggled as she set the tray down. "Word about town is that you should take more time to lie about. I hear you work far too many hours."

"I was filling my time. Too many thoughts I wished to avoid."

Caroline froze at this. "You work to avoid your thoughts?" she finally asked in a hoarse voice.

"I did. But now I plan to turn over a new leaf."

"Why?"

"Why do I plan to make changes?"

She shook her head, a couple of strands of silky hair coming loose from her nape. "No. What thoughts did you wish to avoid?"

William soughed, lifting a hand to rub over his beard. How did he explain his past?

"I had a younger cousin. My uncle, the blacksmith before me, was his father."

"Had?"

William nodded. "Charles and I went to fight Napoleon together." It was strange to explain this to her, after the dream where she had interrupted him at Waterloo.

"He died?"

"He did. His parents were devastated."

"What about you? How did you feel?"

William huffed humorlessly. It was exactly the kind of question he would expect from the perceptive woman who had invaded his dreams the night before. "He was my closest friend, and I watched him die."

Caroline stared at him, licking her lips and clearly uncertain how to respond. Finally, she crossed over to sit down next to him on the settee, placing her smaller hand over his. "I am sorry."

"You have brought me more comfort than you could possibly comprehend."

"Me?"

"Every night since his death, I have dreamed of Charles. When you told me to count my blessings last night … the dream changed. I realized how much my cousin sacrificed so that he might secure freedom for his parents, his town. His country. By focusing on the loss, I failed to honor him. Now I know I must live my life as a mark of respect to Charles. If our positions were reversed … I would want him to have sought a full life. Live life for the both of us."

Caroline stared down at their clasped hands.

"You are a good man, William. You deserve to live a full life."

William broke the clasp to take her in his arms. Embracing her close to bury his face in her hair, he breathed in the scent of vanilla with a hint of peppermint. "What have you brought us to eat?"

She chuckled against him. "I have a roasted chicken and a Christmas mince pie I fetched from the baker, Mr. Andrews."

"What? No Christmas pudding?"

Caroline giggled. "I had no time nor reason to start making a Christmas pudding back in November, I am afraid."

William soughed heavily in feigned disappointment. When she pulled back, he gave her an exaggerated wink. "We shall make do, I suppose."

She smiled, then leaned over the tray, handing him a plate

laden with chicken and pie. "To make matters worse, we have to eat on the settee."

Taking up a fork from the tray, William took a bite of the pie and shut his eyes in bliss. "Mr. Andrews is a genius."

Caroline took her bite, then hummed in delight, which reminded William of her vivid nocturnal visits. Somehow, in his dreams, he had seen to the very essence of this woman and he knew her better than he knew himself. She had found the keys to his cage and released him from purgatory itself.

He only wished he knew her secrets. What would it take to convince her to relinquish the one she was holding back? Perhaps it did not signify. Eventually, he would learn everything about her.

He put his plate down, along with his fork.

Caroline tilted her head in question, but William said nothing. He simply took her plate and fork away to place them beside his own.

Carefully, he lowered himself onto his knee and turned to take her hand with his. Her mouth fell open, her eyes wide as she stared back at him in shock.

"Caroline Brown, will you do me the honor of becoming my wife?"

CHAPTER EIGHT: THE ARGUMENT

"*H*ave you gone mad?" Her question was sincere. She was genuinely concerned that William had lost his mind. "You barely know me!"

"I know everything that matters," he responded, his blue eyes earnest as he cradled her hand in his own. His fingers and palms were rough against her skin, reminding her of the work he did. He built things, bending metal into shapes that would allow it to become useful implements. He did it well, and he had built a business that was the envy of many townsfolk.

And he is offering to marry me?

"Is this because we lay together? You need not feel obligated. I was aware of what I was doing, and I had no expectations of you."

William chuckled. "Nay, Caroline. You are a fine woman, and laying with you would have made me feel obligated to behave as a gentleman, but the truth is, I had already determined this course before we lay together."

"What?"

"I lay with you because I had already decided I wanted to make you my wife."

Caroline's mind was swimming, a maelstrom of confusion. No man had ever desired to marry her before, and from what she knew of the blacksmith, he was not a lunatic. She recalled imagining what it would be like to marry him, but never expected that he desired to do so.

"You do not know me!"

"I know what matters. You are an admirable woman, and it would be my great honor to wed you."

Caroline's heart stopped in her chest. But he did not know her, not truly. He did not know what she had done. Why she was here in Chatternwell. He did not know that her benefactor was Lord Saunton, who had loaned her the funds for her shop and the services of his man of business. And he did not know why Lord Saunton had done these things. What she had done to Miss Annabel. She should not have accepted Lord Saunton's offer of amends for their mutual past mistakes. Culpability lay squarely on her shoulders, but she had selfishly grabbed the opportunity to set herself back on the path that she and Miss Annabel had dreamed and chattered about as children.

She could never share these secrets with William. His esteem had made her feel whole, and she was not willing to ruin it, even if it meant they could no longer be together. If she held his regard, she would at least have the memory of this time with him. If she told him the truth, he would be disgusted, and it would destroy the affinity between them.

William must have sensed something amiss. He squeezed her hand gently. "I apologize for springing this on you. I had intended to … to court you and coax you into accepting me, but I was overcome with the joy of sharing this day with you and wanted it to never end. This decision is not lightly undertaken. I make no decisions lightly."

Caroline raised her free hand to her cheeks to discover they were wet. Tears were streaming down her face. She was at once so flattered, so tempted, yet, on the other hand, terrified.

"What is it, sunshine?" William's expression reflected genuine concern.

"Could we not talk about this now?" She had looked forward to spending these last few hours of Christmas with him before returning to her life. If she turned him down, for there was no other option, it would rob them of their festive enjoyment abruptly. Her eyes were so filled with tears, she could barely see him while her mind raced to find a conclusion.

He picked up a cloth from the table and gently dabbed her cheeks. "Is it so upsetting to contemplate a future with me?"

Caroline shook her head. "It is upsetting to contemplate a future without you."

William gave a deep sigh, his shoulders lifting with the force of it. "I apologize for interrupting our meal. We can discuss this another time. Just … know that the offer stands."

She nodded, the tension easing when he awkwardly raised himself back onto the settee.

Hesitantly, she reached out to pick up her plate while imagining what it would be like to accept his offer. To enjoy dinner with him forevermore. To perhaps have babes of her own to care for. To teach a daughter how to sew or to provide the fictitious child with her first embroidery floss. Caroline stared at the food on her plate, while these future possibilities danced in her head, imagining a little boy with his father's black hair and blue eyes, pulling on the chain with his tiny hand to work the forge bellows while the black-smith held him aloft.

It was so tempting to consider. If only she had not ruined

her future two years earlier when she had broken trust with herself. There could be no idyllic future for a woman keeping shameful secrets—no trusting her to care for others when she had no faith in herself.

Resolutely, she lifted her fork and took a bite of mince pie, taking pains to relish the fruity treat and tear her thoughts away from things that could be nothing but sweet imaginings.

As THEY ATE IN SILENCE, William fought his frustration. He almost missed the deadness of his soul these past years. At least then he had been entirely logical and not driven by impulse or emotions. The success of his business was due to single-minded focus, but he had a hard time recollecting what that had been like since Caroline had reawakened him from the dead and thwarted his careful plans to remain indifferent.

His timing was abysmal. There could be no denying it. He was impatient to hold Caroline at his side, to not let her go. As the time for her to leave drew closer, William felt a desperation to hold on to their magic. To hold on to them.

He had observed she had a secret she had not disclosed, and it had been a terrible miscalculation to ignore what his perception had told him. Proposing marriage while she was inhibited by an unknown burden had been a foolish mistake. All he could do now was distract her to restore their good cheer, so he might try again at a later date.

Chewing on the delicious mince pie, William slowly released his turmoil to enjoy this time with the woman at his side.

"This is the first Christmas I am celebrating in some

years," he finally confessed once his disappointment had settled.

Caroline took a sip of tea before responding, "Because of what happened to your cousin?"

William nodded. "I am pleased to be sharing this day with you."

Her full lips curled into a smile, to his relief. Seeing her cry earlier had been too painful to bear. "As am I."

He smiled in response. "Last year I worked after Christmas service."

She giggled. "So did I! I was the housekeeper for a doctor in Somerset, so we had to take care of the family. Then we celebrated the following day with the feast of Saint Stephen's."

"Yet here we are, together in Chatternwell and eating this pie from Mr. Andrews."

"Here we are."

"I think perhaps this is how I would like to spend every Christmas." He held his breath after he said it. What would she say to that?

Caroline stared down at her plate, seconds ticking by before she answered. "I would like that, too."

William blinked, caught unprepared at this admission. Keeping a straight face, nevertheless, he was overjoyed to hear that she might consider doing that. It was a step in the right direction.

* * *

Do not encourage his attentions!

He deserved much better than herself, but Caroline could not help grasping onto the possibility that come next year, she would come to visit him.

If William were still single then, as she certainly would be, it would be heavenly to rejoin him in this festive fantasy. When she left this evening, she could hold on to the promise of their reunion. When she awoke alone in her bed, and the old memories threatened to eat her alive, she could turn her thoughts to this promise of a future respite.

When they finished eating, she offered him a second helping, which he accepted. Taking their plates to the back, she fondly replenished his plate. A large man like him evidently needed much more food than she. Chuckling, she carefully laid out some choice pieces of chicken and placed mince pie next to them. She hummed while pouring more tea, then returned to the sitting room with a full tray, which she set down.

Moving about the room, she straightened up pillows and stoked the fire in the hearth. Caroline had grown accustomed to his home, and it was depressing to think she would leave soon to return to her silent rooms.

"Do you have someone to take care of you in the morning?"

William stretched his neck, rubbing his shoulder before responding, "One of my apprentices should come to find me. I am hoping Dr. Hadley will give me permission to walk when he comes to visit in the morning. The swelling has reduced a fair amount, so I hope that a second examination from him will reveal that the sprain was not as terrible as we first thought."

Caroline wandered over, bending to peer at his ankle before feeling about gently with her fingers. "It certainly is better than when I first arrived."

He nodded, then said, hesitantly, "If you sit with me, I can read to you."

She took her seat next to him, and he reached for the book he had laid on the table. "What will you read me?"

"It is Christmas, so I thought I would read you verses from popular wassails."

Throwing out an arm, he pulled her close into the crook of it to lean his head on hers. Reaching around her, he held the little book open and recited the blessing out loud, sending shivers of warm delight through her body.

> *Huzza, Huzza, in our good town*
> *The bread shall be white, and the liquor be brown*
> *So here my old fellow I drink to thee*
> *And the very health of each other tree.*
> *Well may ye blow, well may ye bear*
> *Blossom and fruit both apple and pear.*
> *So that every bough and every twig*
> *May bend with a burden both fair and big*
> *May ye bear us and yield us fruit such a stors*
> *That the bags and chambers and house run o'er.*

As he finished and turned the page to find another, Caroline's eyes drifted shut so she might listen to the crackle of the fire, the beating in his chest, and the timbre of his deep voice.

This is what true happiness must feel like.

Soon it would end, but she had the promise of returning to celebrate again with him next year. Christmas could not come too soon once she left him behind to return to work.

* * *

AFTER READING FOR SOME TIME, William finished and reluctantly shut the book.

Caroline slowly opened her eyes and sat up, forcing him to relinquish his embrace. "I suppose I must replace your poultice, provide you some supplies, and then head home."

Her usually cheerful voice had a sad intonation as she rubbed her eyes.

William licked his lips, wishing he could prolong their time together. "Do you have to leave so soon?"

"I am not sure when my landlady will return, and I should be there when she arrives to prevent questions about where I have been."

His throat thickened with emotion as she stood and moved away. Their time was ending, and the only promise he had secured was that she would return a year from now.

The intelligence he had applied to building his business was nowhere to be found as desperation to hold on to the time with her as long as he could bit deep.

"What if I courted you? Would that be acceptable?"

Caroline's expression crumpled. Had she been upset about leaving if her emotions were so close to the surface?

"Please trust me when I say that you do not wish to pursue me. I am not worthy, William."

He rubbed a hand over his chin, trying to think. "I believe you are."

She shook her head. "But I am not. You do not know what I have done."

William's interest piqued at this declaration. Her secret had to do with something she felt culpable for? Perhaps if he could persuade her to tell him her shame, he could convince her to consider the blessings she must be ignoring. She had helped him to reconsider the past and find solace. Perhaps he could do the same for her.

"Please come take a seat?"

She walked over, sitting down with a thump at his side. "If I could, I would stay, William."

"Can you tell me why you feel you are not suitable for my attentions? Perhaps if you explain it to me, it will not seem so insurmountable."

Her hands came together as she fidgeted in agitation. "If I tell you what I did, I will lose your regard, and I do not want that."

He brought a hand over hers to provide comfort. "Please, sunshine. There is nothing you could say to change my mind about you."

Caroline's shoulders shook as she swallowed a sob. "It was unforgivable."

"Nothing is unforgivable if one makes an effort to correct it."

"There is no fixing what I have done."

William tugged on his beard, trying to think what to say. "Nevertheless, whatever you tell me will never change my mind about the woman who took care of me on Christmas Eve."

Her head lifted, her eyes finding his. The torment in their depths was enough to break his heart, but he did not flinch. He needed to be steady, so he returned her gaze and lifted a hand to tuck a lock of hair behind her ear. She was so achingly beautiful, and he must show her strength if he was to convince her to change her mind.

"When I was thirteen, my grandmother died. She was my only living relation."

He nodded, but his chest tightened at these words. She had been only a year or two older than when his own parents had left this earth. Fortunately, he had Uncle Albert to take him in.

"Mrs. Harris had known my grandmother, and she promised she would provide me a position when I needed it. So I went to work at Baydon Hall, where she was the house-keeper." Caroline fell silent, so William reached out a hand to caress the curve of her cheek in encouragement. "Miss Annabel was a little younger than me. The daughter of a baron. She took the time to teach me to read and how to do numbers. When she learned I was adept at sewing, she provided me with fabrics and convinced Mrs. Harris to apprentice me. We discussed me opening dress-rooms one day, and she vowed to invest her pin money when she was married to help me." Caroline choked up.

William put an arm around her in comfort, and she turned her head into his shoulder to hide her face. "What did you do?"

"The Earl of Saunton began courting Miss Annabel when she was nineteen. Soon they announced they were to marry, and he was visiting all the time, and I ... we ... I ... I gave him my virtue!"

He held her tight as she broke into sobs, stroking her back to calm her. "You blame yourself for behaving in an improper manner?"

She shook her head against him, her voice muffled when she finally replied, "Nay, William, for betraying my dear friend. Miss Annabel did so much to help me, and I ruthlessly deceived her."

William tried to imagine himself in Caroline's position. What if he had stolen Nellie from his cousin when they were younger? He admitted that the guilt of it would have eaten him alive, so he understood the distress she felt.

"What happened?"

Caroline sobbed before eventually answering the question. "She caught us. In the stables."

Bloody hell, he felt terrible on her behalf. She was clearly still distraught over the situation after all this time. But how much time was it?

"She provided me a reference and had Mrs. Harris find me the position with the doctor."

Well ... that was unexpectedly generous. Caroline might not be overstating their friendship if the young woman had seen to her future despite her anger.

"And did she marry the Earl of Saunton?" Lord Saunton had a country estate nearby, and he had married recently, but William was not sure whom he had married.

"Nay, Miss Annabel married the Duke of Halmesbury."

William's head snapped up. "The duke? From here in Wiltshire?"

"Yes. You know of His Grace?"

"Of course! His country seat is just two hours south of Chatternwell. But, Caroline, did Miss Annab—Her Grace refuse your apology?"

Caroline buried her face even deeper into his shoulder, hesitating for several seconds before admitting in a muffled voice, "I never apologized."

"Why?"

"She sent me away, and I never had the opportunity."

"Have you tried to write to her or obtain an audience since then?"

"No, but ... she would not want to see me."

William considered her words and realized he had been in a similar situation to Caroline. Locked in his regrets over Charles, he had lost all perspective. "Why does this prevent you from accepting my courtship?"

"I vowed I would not form any connections after what I did. I cannot be trusted. No one should trust me, least of all a husband. What if I betrayed you?"

William frowned in confusion. "When did this happen?"

"Two years ago."

"And have you done anything similar?"

"No. I cannot be trusted." Caroline repeated the earlier words as if she were reciting lines. As if she had told herself these words on too many occasions and truly come to believe them. She was an intelligent young woman when it came to her business, or to helping others. But, like him, she was irrational when it came to herself and her own worth.

"Then I stand by what I said. You made a single mistake, and I do not believe you will do so again, given that you have refrained from all personal connections since it happened. I remain committed to my desire to court you."

Caroline raised her head to stare at him. "My character does not repulse you?"

"I am not repulsed. We have all made mistakes, and you regret yours deeply. I will not hold them against you when you have shown me such kindness." Was she truly unaware of what a marvel she was? She had taken Annie Greer under her wing, and provided the little girl with coin when she needed it most. Annie was learning a useful trade for her future. Not to mention that Caroline had risked her reputation to nurse him on Christmas Eve and, with her words, had rescued him from the shadows. He had to help her let go of the past, as she had helped him to do. "I wish to court you, sunshine."

He could see she was thinking about it, his mouth growing dry with nervous anticipation. Now that she had confessed the truth and received his heartfelt reassurance, would she relent on her vow? Seconds stretched into minutes as her feelings flittered across her features, and William bit his lip to remain silent and not interrupt as she tried to reach a decision.

"I cannot." Her words cracked the silence, a deafening blow. William's free hand came up to his chest, certain he would find it cracked open and bleeding his life essence. He had awoken from years of being half dead, to fall violently in love over the span of a few hours, only to have his esteem rejected.

Surely his heart had physically snapped in two?

Releasing her, he tried to think what to say next. Lifting a hand, he rubbed it over his beard, quelling the urge to tear at his hair in his desolation.

To make matters worse, he suspected he was being selfish.

He had found a lifeline to happiness and grabbed it with both hands, hauling himself to shore with all his strength. But what of Caroline? What of her needs? She was in agony over what she had done to her mistress, and he could only commiserate, being well aware of how guilt could cut through one's soul to leave one broken and bleeding. To be certain that there was nothing left to live for, not a solitary blessing to cling to.

With great reluctance, William admitted what she needed. And currently it was not him. The only possible step to take was to release her.

It was the hardest thing he had ever done, other than witness Charles's death, but he did it regardless. Because Caroline needed him to do it and he could not possibly achieve his future dream of them together without putting her first. No matter how long it took, he would eventually bring them back together. But only if he allowed them to part first.

He lay back, fighting his instincts to do what was right. "I … understand."

Caroline looked as if she had been slapped. She blinked several times, then cleared her throat before standing up. "All right, then. I am … glad you understand."

William nodded, closing his eyes so he would not leap up to grab hold of her. She paused, hesitating for several seconds, before finally speaking once more. "I shall collect my things and go home."

She paused again as if expecting him to disagree, but he bit his tongue and remained silent. He had rushed matters between them, and he needed to retreat before he made it worse.

"Goodbye … William."

He gave a curt nod, bidding himself to remain calm and release her from any obligations to him. It was his only hope, and he did not trust himself to speak.

CHAPTER NINE: THE TRUTH

*C*aroline was bent over the walking dress when she heard Annie approaching the shop. It lifted her flagging spirits that she would have company today, so she paused to cock her head and listen to the carol.

> *The twelfth day of Christmas,*
> *My true love sent to me,*
> *Twelve lords a leaping,*
> *Eleven ladies dancing,*
> *Ten pipers piping,*
> *Nine drummers drumming,*
> *Eight maids a milking,*

The back door opened, and the singing was no longer muffled as Annie drew a deep breath to complete the lengthy verse in her sweet, youthful voice.

Seven swans a swimming,
Six geese a laying,
Five gold rings,
Four colly birds,
Three French hens,
Two turtle doves, and
A partridge in a pear tree.

Annie walked over to the worktable where Caroline was seated and finished her song with a flourish, clearly proud of herself for recalling all the lines correctly. "Happy Saint Stephen's Day, Mrs. Brown!"

Caroline forced a cheery smile on her tired face. She had been depressed since leaving the blacksmith's home the day before and had not slept a wink all night. Considering how their time together had ended, she did not know what to make of their relationship. Did they even have one after she had rejected his suit?

"Happy Saint Stephen's Day, Annie!"

The child gave a little curtsy then asked a question that must have been bothering her. "What is a colly bird, Mrs. Brown?"

"Colly means black, like coal."

"Oh. So the fourth day is about blackbirds?"

"It would seem so. The song is originally French, so there may be mistakes in the translation, but I think blackbirds sound correct."

"And why do you think so many days are about birds, but not the fifth day?"

She shrugged. "They say perhaps the gold rings are gold ring-necked pheasants. I have not personally seen one, but they are quite colorful from what I am told."

Annie nodded, her attention flitting away to light on a different subject as children were wont to do.

"We had a wonderful Christmas feast. Mr. Andrews joined us after closing his shop, and Mum made you some black butter." Annie placed a little pot on the table. Caroline picked it up and opened it to look inside at the fruit paste, sniffing the distinctive scent with pleasure.

"Tell your mum thank you. I shall buy some fresh bread to eat it with!"

Annie nodded before collecting her apron and tying it on. "I think Mr. Andrews is sweet on Mum. He has invited us to go wassailing on Twelfth Night."

Caroline gritted her teeth in exasperation. Fantastic! Mrs. Greer would secure a new husband, whereas Caroline would remain alone forever while a perfectly good man lay, rejected, on his settee down the street. Not just any man—William. She missed him something fierce since leaving his home.

Have I made the right decision?

Realizing she had not responded to Annie's announcement, she forced a cheery tone and asked the important question. "How do you feel about that?"

Annie stopped to consider her answer, her little face pensive. "I think Mr. Andrews is a jolly man. And he makes excellent food, so I suppose it would be all right if he courts Mum."

Caroline chuckled, the first time she had been inclined to do so all day. "Excellent food will always be acceptable."

Annie grinned back. "I shall fetch your bread for you if you like. Mr. Andrews might be inclined to give me a Sally Lunn bun if I visit his shop."

"Then I have no choice. I shall have to allow you to run the errand for me. Tell Mr. Andrews to put it on my account."

"Shall I sweep the front?"

"Yes. I want to work on my walking dress, and I expect

little custom today. When you finish in the front, you can come sit with me and I will show you what I am doing."

The girl nodded and walked through the workroom door before racing back with a worried expression. "Mrs. Brown! Some of the Christmas boughs are missing!"

A nervous agitation tightened her stomach as Caroline realized she had forgotten to bring back the boughs. After the abrupt end to her day with William, she had simply left without them. "I … gave them to someone who needed them more than me." She needed to distract Annie before she asked any further questions. "Did you complete the handkerchief you were sewing?"

The girl looked down, her expression guilty as she mumbled her response. "No … I was too busy helping Mum make the Christmas boughs."

"You can join me when you are done sweeping and finish it then."

Annie brightened up. It had been a shameful manipulation on Caroline's part in an effort to change the subject, but it would not do to have anyone asking questions about how she had spent Christmas.

* * *

WILLIAM HAD CONVINCED Dr. Hadley that he was recovered enough to be back on his feet. The doctor had bound his ankle, cautioning him to be careful and not over-exert himself, but had concurred that the sprain was not as severe as it had appeared on Christmas Eve.

Then he had requested to use the doctor's carriage, to which the doctor had also agreed, but they had haggled for some time. Dr. Hadley had not wanted to charge him for the favor, while William had insisted that he must pay a rental fee. Eventually, they had struck a mutually agreeable bargain, and the doctor had left to order his carriage be readied.

Saint Stephen's Day was the perfect time to call on a lady of means. It was a day of charity, and well-to-do households opened their doors to their community. William was going to take advantage of the festive traditions to assist Caroline.

He was committed to helping her heal, because she had helped him to heal. She had brought much-needed comfort to him, freed him from the traumatic day at the Hougoumont farmhouse, and he could not let her down.

Eventually she would forgive him, he hoped, for his clumsy interference in her life—if he succeeded in his quest.

William washed up in haste, but took his time with his attire. He donned a pristine white shirt before pulling on his finest stockings and best breeches, the ones reserved for church and special occasions. Then he polished his buckled shoes, grimacing at the thought of wearing them, but they were the only ones he could. Not only were they more elegant than his boots, but he could not get a boot on with his ankle bandaged.

Then he tied a cravat, donned a navy wool tailcoat, and finally collected his hat. It was imperative that he be well-received where he was going. As much as he disliked dressing formally, he would do whatever it took to bring about Caroline's cessation from her suffering.

CAROLINE WORKED on the walking dress she had spent so many months on, but it did not bring solace. Her magical holiday interlude was done. Nothing more than a memory to hold dear. She feared she had greatly disappointed the blacksmith, and the more she thought about it, the less sense it made to have walked away.

But, then, he had abruptly changed his mind and allowed her to do so. Perhaps he had time to consider her failings and lost interest in pursuing her.

Annie came in from sweeping the front. Fetching her needles and some floss, she came to take a seat next to Caroline by the worktable.

"You do not appear to be in good spirits, Mrs. Brown?"

"I am sad that Christmas is over," she offered by way of explanation.

Annie twisted her mouth in genuine perplexment at Caroline's statement. The girl evidently suspected she had lost her senses. "Christmastide is not over. It only ends on Twelfth Night. There are many celebrations ahead."

Caroline's hand froze as she absorbed the simplicity of Annie's statement. Children were so straightforward. There was no complexity to their ideas, and somehow this shined a light on the events of the past two days. Why was she at work pining for William when he had accepted her with all her faults and offered her an honorable future together? Why could she not reconsider her vow in light of her change of circumstances?

Biting her lip, she feared her decision had been driven by … well … fear.

It was not too late. Perhaps … she could simply take a chance on herself. Punishing herself might not be the best answer when a man as generous and kind as William wanted to offer her a full life.

Of course, if she were to allow him to court her, she would need to admit where she had gained the funds for her shop. She shut her eyes in distress. How had she not imparted that information while she was confessing her sins? Could she admit how she came to own a shop in Chatternwell? Would he be repelled to learn that her former paramour had given her the funds, and consider her to be a kept woman, or would he believe her that it was a loan to be repaid and only advanced as compensation for past misdeeds?

Why not visit him and see where the conversation takes you?

She dithered, staring down at her needlework while she tried to reach a decision.

"I have an errand to run. Can you mind the shop for an hour, or should I close it?"

Annie raised her eyebrows in surprise but did not question her. "I can mind the shop. There is not much custom today."

Caroline put her work down on the table and rose. She swiftly put her things away and hung the gown back in its place of honor until she had time to work on it again. If William proved understanding, perhaps she could wear it to her wedding one day.

Donning her cloak, the one that he had teased her about, Caroline exited from the back and hurried down the alleyway. When she reached the block where William's cottage was, she stopped and looked about. There were too many people about on the streets. She could not approach his home without being seen. And if Mrs. Heeley was back from Bath, Caroline would be spotted for certain.

She nibbled on her lip, realizing she had been loitering too long. Someone was going to notice her awkwardly standing about. She turned up the cross street to re-enter Market Street, as she strived for a solution. She could try the smithy. William had said he was hoping the doctor would confirm his ankle was in better condition than the initial examination. Perhaps he had gone to work.

Caroline headed toward the bellowing chimneys of the smithy, folding her cloak closer as a winter wind hit her and blew right up her sleeves to chill her arms with its icy grip. Perhaps William was right about it. Perhaps she could make a second cloak for colder days such as this and keep the pretty but ineffective one for milder weather.

As she approached the smithy, it soon became clear it was in full operation. The shutters were flung open to allow the cold breeze to dissipate the heat from the forges, and the sound of hammers beating down on metal produced a cacophony of clanging.

She entered through the customer door and came to a stop at the counter that separated the waiting area from the long work area. It was her first time visiting the smithy, but it was clear William ran an impressive operation. There were three forges with giant bellows hanging behind their chimneys, and with one or two men around each forge using tongs to heat black iron to a cherry red.

An apprentice was sweeping up, while another was raking the shards of coal neatly into a pile on one of the waist-high forges. Another had his hand high above his head, pulling on a handle attached to a chain to work the bellows which heated the coals.

Three or four journeymen worked at anvils braced onto wooden stumps, hammering at red-hot metal to produce a clanging so loud, she brought her fingers up to stop her ears.

On the counter, there were large catalogs to peruse, one of locks and another of farming tools, and on the wall was a display of locks and tools for purchase, neatly hung for customers to look at. A section dedicated to steel included especially fine work, and she concluded that these would be the items which brought the largest profits for the smithy.

A boy of about fifteen caught sight of her. Leaning his broom against a wall, he hurried over to assist her, wiping his hands on his leather apron as he approached. She removed her fingers from her ears.

"Can I help you, ma'am?"

"I was looking for Mr. Jackson. Is he here today?"

"No, ma'am. He took the day to travel to Bath. Something about visiting someone on Saint Stephen's Day."

One of the men at the nearest forge overheard. Throwing a look over his shoulder, he guffawed loudly. "More like gone a-courting, dressed in his Sunday finest."

Several men broke out laughing, joking about how the blacksmith was sweet on someone in Bath.

All Caroline could think of was how unbearably inconvenient it was to realize she was in love with William at the precise moment she learned she had lost him. Swallowing the lump in her throat, she fought back the sting of tears while struggling for her composure.

She had lost her opportunity. The man had wanted to marry her yesterday. Perhaps when she had disappointed him, he had sought a new interest.

Work, Caroline. You can work.

She pulled in a thready breath, grateful the deafening sounds of the smithy masked her pain. The boy at the counter cocked his head quizzically. "Are you all right, ma'am?"

"Fine. I am fine. Mr. Jackson was speaking with me about … repairing a lock. I will return tomorrow."

Caroline swept away before the apprentice could reply. She needed to get away before she revealed her emotions.

Turning back to Market Street, she walked the length, passing her shop without pausing. Her legs carried her without direction from her brain while she attempted to come to terms with the idea that she had possibly—probably —lost William when she had left his home the day before. If he was courting someone in her place, she did not even have the promise of next Christmas to cling to.

Icy wind tunneled around the nearby buildings to blast her as she fought for control over her emotions. Perhaps the men had misunderstood? William did not seem a fickle man.

He had assured her that the offer to wed stood. If only she could talk to him and sort this out.

But how could she? Now that Christmas Day was over, their street was bustling again. Attempting to sneak into his home to discuss it was fraught with potential consequences. Not to mention, she did not know when he would return.

She should never have allowed herself to grow close to him. It was a mistake to form connections. Connections could be lost and then all one had were the ashes of regret. She should have clung to her work, which had kept her sane these past two years. Breaking her vow had brought fresh pain to contend with.

Work is the answer!

CHAPTER TEN: THE RECONCILIATION

THE FIFTH DAY OF CHRISTMAS

She had not caught a glimpse of the blacksmith in several days, but there he was, across the street entering the post office. If she hurried out there, she could catch him on his way out and determine once and for all if she had lost her opportunity.

Over the past three days, since visiting the smithy and learning he was gone to Bath, Caroline had worked under a shroud of turmoil. One moment she was committed to working, the next she was wondering, what if?

What if William was not courting another woman? What if this was a misunderstanding, and his offer to wed was still valid? What if they could form a wonderful union, two successful proprietors united in a partnership? Assist each other in realizing their respective dreams?

For the first time in days, she might have an opportunity to find out where matters stood.

"I think perhaps I would like to see the blue silk again."

NINA JARRETT

"Miss Jolie, Lady Jolie, would you mind if my apprentice assisted you for just a moment? I see someone I must converse with, but I will be right back."

The young woman and her mother nodded, still fingering the fabrics they were inspecting. Caroline brought out the silk they had requested while calling for Annie, keeping a nervous eye out for William to ensure she did not miss him, before hurrying out the front door.

Crossing the street, she stopped outside the post office, fidgeting with her gown while she tried to decide if she should follow him in. Leaving her shop without a cloak had been ill-advised—she was quickly growing cold in the winter air, but if she entered, they could hardly speak of anything meaningful.

Just as she raised her hand to enter, she saw William approaching from the other side of the door and stepped back to allow him to exit. He caught sight of her through the glass panes and appeared to hesitate for a moment, as if he were preparing himself before he opened the door and strode out.

"Mrs. Brown, season's greetings." His words were polite, but the intonation was flat, as if he were parodying appropriate behavior.

Caroline gave a slight curtsy in greeting. "Mr. Jackson, I … wanted to discuss that lock." She glanced restlessly toward the two women passing by behind him. William stared over her shoulder, refusing to meet her eyes.

Realizing William would not look at her, Caroline's heart sank. So it was true. William had moved on after her rejection. He had found someone who would appreciate him, which she had failed to do.

"However, it is not urgent. I shall visit you at the smithy when I have time." She stepped back, her hopes and what-ifs finally dashed to pieces like the waves hitting rocks in the seascape over his mantel. Which she would never see again, not these holidays or the next.

William put out a hand as if to stay her. "Mrs. Brown, I—" He stopped, his eyes focused on a point over her shoulder. It was clear he had been about to say something, but now he stood taciturn, even unnerved. Behind her, she could hear the rumble of wheels. "—I must go!"

With that, he abruptly turned to storm down the street. Caroline was left to watch his retreating form until she was distracted by how loud the approaching vehicle was.

Frowning, she turned around to see what had caught his attention and discovered that a large, ornate carriage was approaching. Liveried servants could be seen in blue with gold brocade. Someone important must be visiting Chatternwell.

Realizing she had left Miss Jolie and her mother alone with Annie and a promise to return, Caroline quickly crossed the street to re-enter her shop. The warmth was a relief, even if it could not warm her frozen heart.

"Miss Jolie, my apologies. I … had a lock that needed repair, and Mr. Jackson happened to be passing by."

"It is no trouble, Mrs. Brown. I shall have the gown made with the Saxon blue silk, if you could?"

Caroline blinked in surprise. It was one of her most expensive fabrics, so the order would include substantial profit. It appeared that her business would continue to thrive while inside she floundered. She nodded, pulling out her order book to write down the young woman's instructions.

Shortly, the two women exited the shop, chattering about a visit to the haberdashery next door. Which was when Caroline realized that the elegant carriage she had seen approaching earlier had stopped in front of her shop and a footman stood at attention next to its gilded door.

Lady Jolie and Miss Jolie paused, peering curiously at

the carriage. It was the finest Caroline had ever seen, with an intricate coat of arms on the door, luxurious drapery in the windows, and a gilded finial at the crest of the slanting roof.

The footman continued to stand at attention, paying no mind to the two women gawking at him. Eventually, they moved off, casting inquisitive glances over their shoulders as they walked away.

Caroline was transfixed, staring at the carriage. As soon as the two women disappeared from sight, the footman sprang into action as if he had been awaiting their departure. He reached up to open the carriage door, then fixed the steps in place before stepping aside.

Highly polished black riding boots came into view on the top step, followed by buckskins draped over powerful legs, and then a man descended. A very large, Viking of a man, several inches over six feet, with blond hair and an elegant blue tailcoat.

Caroline blinked rapidly, trying to place him, before her mouth fell open. It was the Duke of Halmesbury!

The earl had briefly introduced them back in August when she had visited Lord Saunton at Chatternwell House to sign her loan documents.

The duke turned and held up a hand to assist a woman to descend from the dim interior. All Caroline could make out was the expensive hem of a burgundy carriage dress, the duke blocking most of her view, but blood began to pound loudly in her ears.

There could only be one woman who would accompany the duke in the ducal carriage. Caroline was about to meet her past.

"Annie!" The girl came running from the back, clearly alarmed at the sharpness of her employer's voice.

"Yes, Mrs. Brown?"

Caroline drew a breath to modulate her tone. "Please run over to Mr. Andrews and purchase some pies for us."

Annie's brown eyes brightened in anticipation. A visit to Mr. Andrews was certain to earn her a sticky bun. "Yes, Mrs. Brown."

As the child turned away, Caroline called out, "And, Annie, take your time. I need to meet with this customer in private."

Annie nodded vigorously, more than happy to have some time to herself as she skipped to the back. Fortunately, Mrs. Jones and her daughter were not working today, so Caroline had the shop to herself. And her unexpected guest.

Outside, the duke stepped aside to reveal his wife. Miss Annabel, chestnut hair neatly coifed and brandy eyes shining, sought her out through the windowpanes. Caroline flushed as their gazes met, licking her lips and wiping her damp palms over her skirts to still their trembling while Her Grace approached the door.

The footman opened it, stepping back to allow the duchess entry and then shutting the door behind her. This was to be a private audience.

Caroline and Her Grace stared at each other across the shop for several seconds before Caroline recalled her place and sank into a deep curtsy. "Miss Anna—Your Grace."

The young woman laughed out loud. "No matter how long I am married to the duke, I never grow accustomed to how old acquaintances behave because of my increased station as his wife. It is"—the duchess tilted her head as if seeking the right word—"disconcerting."

"My apologies, Your Grace."

The duchess walked over to where Caroline was awkwardly posed in the curtsy, uncertain if she was to rise in these circumstances. "I have come to visit an old friend, so perhaps you should rise and we can converse freely."

Caroline choked as she returned to a standing position and rubbed at her dry throat. When she regained the ability to speak, she sputtered, "Old friend?"

Her Grace tilted her head again, contemplating her with a sad expression. "Were we not friends?"

Her throat muscles worked, and eventually Caroline croaked her response. "Until I ruined it."

"Hmm."

"What are you doing here?" Caroline clapped a hand over her mouth at the shrill demand. "Your Grace," she added in an attempt to soften her high-strung tone.

"I received a visit from a Mr. Jackson on Saint Stephen's Day. He told me you were in dire need of an audience with me. He seemed to think that I was a woman of noble character who would be magnanimous if I were to understand your troubles."

Caroline's eyes widened in horror. To do such a thing! Rage rose as a heavy feeling in her head, making her feel giddy from the force of it. The Sunday finest! He had not been to Bath to court a lass. He had been to Avonmead to visit the duchess!

William was rude, insufferable, arrogant, invasive, and … and …

"Sweet? Loyal? Determined to secure your happiness?" the duchess responded.

Caroline clapped a hand over her mouth again. Had she spoken the words out loud?

"You did. What struck me during his visit was that you must care deeply about this man if you shared your secret with him. I was very pleased to discover that a man of such quality had taken it upon himself to speak on your behalf, but grew concerned when he informed me that his offer to marry you had been declined because of our shared history. Which is why I agreed to visit you. I would have come earlier, but this is the first day of Christmastide that did not have specific obligations to attend to."

Caroline nodded. Yesterday had been the Feast of the Innocents, and the day before had been the Feast of Saint John the Evangelist. As her thoughts skittered about inanely, Caroline realized she was procrastinating due to shock. Ransacking her mind, she located her senses to finally say something that was … not deplorable. "I have long wanted … to apologize for my actions."

The duchess nodded, setting her rich red-brown curls to bouncing. "This conversation is overdue." She turned and walked away to inspect the shop, before coming to a stop by the door and glancing about to take it all in at once. "The shop is exactly as we imagined it as girls."

"I thought of you often when I was preparing it for opening."

Her Grace turned her head to gaze at her directly. "I have thought of you often, too. I was very pleased when I heard that Lord Saunton had taken responsibility for you and was financing our plans in my stead."

Caroline inhaled in surprise. "You were? Why?"

"I never wished you ill. Your actions precluded us from continuing on together, and I will admit I was furious for a few weeks, but then my situation changed. What happened between us … it led me to the duke. If I had not caught you and Lord Saunton together, we would be unhappily married, but instead I am married to a wonderful man whom I needed. Who needed me. Now we have a strong young boy we both adore."

Caroline slumped as she listened to this declaration, tears stinging in threat of a bout of weeping. "It is so comforting to hear I did not ruin your life!"

The duchess frowned. "Ruined my life, no. Lord Saunton

was the very worst of rakes until he met his wife. We would have had a disastrous marriage."

Caroline swiped the tears from her lashes with a trembling hand. "I am so happy for you … truly … but … hearing that … why do I still feel guilt? It's been two years, and the shame has not worn off."

Her Grace said nothing, contemplating the question until she sighed heavily. "Lord Saunton informed me he had to release the guilt. That it was not about what I thought of him, but what he thought of himself. He had to make reparations to the women he had wronged to reach a point where he could trust himself."

"I do not understand."

"It is not my place to forgive you. Forgiveness must come from within. None of us are free of mistakes, so you will have to find a way to come to terms with what you did."

"I do not know how!" cried Caroline, feeling desperate to be so close to resolution yet still not finding what she was seeking.

The duchess walked forward, stopping before Caroline to take up her hands with her own and stare into her eyes. Caroline was enthralled by the warm gold and brown striations, unable to look away.

"Why did you do it?"

"I was so lonely. No man had ever paid attention to me before, and Lord Saunton was … charming and solicitous."

"Be that as it may, what was the cost to your self-respect?"

Caroline shook her head. "Far beyond what I would be willing to pay if I was presented with similar circumstances in the future."

"So you have considered your mistakes and learned from them?"

"I have."

"And now I have assured you there was no lasting damage, and it all worked out for the best."

"Which is gratifying to hear."

"Then what do we do to restore your faith in yourself?"

"I suppose ... speaking with you is the first step. I was initially angry when you told me Mr. Jackson had manipulated this meeting, but now ... I needed to see you to express my regret."

Miss Annabel nodded. "When I heard how deeply concerned Mr. Jackson was for your happiness ... He is a good man."

Caroline bit her lip, thinking about what came next. What could she do to ease her guilt? She had taken pains to not repeat her past, and the duchess said it had all turned out for the best, which was very good to hear, but still ... She needed to offer some token of her regret.

Nay! Not a token of my regret, but rather a token of my esteem to demonstrate how much I value our shared past!

Despite her actions to the contrary, Caroline had always valued her connection to Miss Annabel and Mrs. Harris. She needed to express her love and appreciation for everything they had done to secure her current success. For leading Caroline to her dreams. For teaching her strength.

But how?

"Could I do something for you? Perhaps ... make you something?" Caroline's hand flew over her mouth once more, mortified at her own words. "I apologize. Of course, you are a duchess and anything I create would be far too inferior!"

The duchess frowned, twin furrows of disapproval appearing between her brows. "Do not disparage yourself. I would be honored to receive a gift from Chatternwell's preeminent modiste."

Modiste!

Until that very moment, Caroline had thought of herself as an audacious maid who had reinvented herself as a dressmaker in a small town. Now she swelled with pride as she considered herself as a fashionable modiste, offering one of her creations to a duchess of the realm. Her mind raced with possibilities as she finally accepted that she was now doing what she was always meant to do. That Her Grace had seen that potential in her as a girl and now visited her to verify her welfare was the revelation she had needed to shift her perspective and accept that this was her role now.

"I could"—Caroline glanced around, frantically searching for an idea fit for a duchess when her eyes landed on the door of the coach out on the road—"present you with a very fine walking dress embroidered with the Halmesbury coat of arms!"

The duchess's eyes widened in surprise before lighting with happiness as she turned to peer out the window at her husband. Silence reigned for several seconds before the duchess turned back, and Caroline saw her dark lashes were glistening with unshed tears. The duke, who was watching from his position outside the window, frowned in inquisitive concern, straightening up to stare pensively into the shop. "That would be unique and highly valued."

Tears of joy sprung into Caroline's eyes, overcome by the dense emotion that filled the room. "I have worked on such a dress for months. I shall personally embroider it. It can be ready for you by tomorrow."

"We are spending the night at Chatternwell House, so I shall speak with the duke about delaying our return until tomorrow afternoon."

Her Grace walked back to the door, the footman springing forward to open it on her behalf. Out on the road, she spoke with her husband in hushed voices before returning.

"His Grace agrees. Shall I try the dress on? The footman will bring you a pillow from the carriage with the coat of arms to use as a template."

"Yes. Thank you … Miss Annabel."

The duchess grinned at this reminder of their shared youth. "My pleasure … Caroline."

Caroline showed the duchess into the back where the gown hung. Gazing up at it, she felt a twinge of regret. Just a few days ago, she had thought about marrying in it, but she quickly pushed that aside. It would be so much more valuable as the key to unlock a future without the substantial burdens of guilt and shame she had carried these past two years. It was a symbol of how far she had come, of her regrets over her mistakes, and the key to a new beginning more profound than the opening of her shop.

"It is exquisite!" proclaimed the noblewoman, fingering it gently.

"The finest velvet I could find. I bought it from the port in London, directly from the merchant who shipped it in."

Caroline took it down and held it out. The duchess divested her carriage dress to reveal an ivory linen gown beneath it, then raising her arms, she slipped them into the walking dress. Buttoning it up, Her Grace went to stand in front of the mirror, posing in different angles. "What do you think of the color? Do you think we suit—your dress and I?"

"You … are utterly beguiling in it. It is as if it was always intended for you."

"And the coat of arms?"

"I shall embroider it with gilt floss onto the back."

"That will be striking against the Prussian blue. This is your finest work."

Caroline examined the garment, draping it around the duchess while she noted what work was needed. "It is, and it is only fitting that I made it for you. I shall let the cuffs out for your longer arms, and re-hem it because you are a little taller, but those appear to be the only adjustments needed. If I work through the night, I can have it ready for you early afternoon."

"Perfect. That will give us time to return to Avonmead before sunset."

Caroline helped Her Grace remove the garment. They returned to the front of the shop, and the duchess made to leave.

"Thank you for taking such trouble to come see me, Your Grace."

"It sets my mind at ease to know you are succeeding. You must have put a lot of work into this." Impulsively, the duchess embraced her. "I am so happy you found someone who appreciates you. Take care of him and do not be too angry with him for interfering."

Caroline nodded, but her attention was on the dress. William would be a matter she dealt with once her work was done. She headed to the back as Annie returned, but she paid no mind, muttering that she had a deadline to see to. All she could think of was how she wanted every ounce of respect and love she felt for Miss Annabel to be reflected in her work. The gratitude she had for all of her years of encouragement. The care she had experienced when she was lost and alone as an orphaned young girl. The regret— *Nay, I refuse to linger on the mistake.*

Taking the gown over to the table by the window, she began working. Annie made tea, which she set on the table, but Caroline pored over the gown without noticing. She worked until her eyeballs were dried-out husks, and her eyelids could not glide over. She moistened them with silver water and then continued until her fingers bled from accumulated pinpricks when she grew too hasty. Dabbing them so as not to stain the cloth, she worked on.

This was about restoring her self-worth by presenting a gift that had her very soul woven into its creation to communicate her love for the best friend she had ever had. By remembering all the good times, the wonderful time spent with the young woman, Caroline energized her body to keep working.

When she was not satisfied, she pulled the floss out to redo the work. This was to be perfection, worthy not just of a duchess but her closest friend, and as the minutes turned into hours, Caroline worked.

To her surprise, the more she toiled, with only brief naps through the course of the night, the better she felt. The black guilt that haunted her, the shadows of self-doubt, melted away until, finally, she raised her head as dawn broke over the hills of Chatternwell. Laying the gown aside, she folded her arms on the table and lowered her head to fall into an exhausted sleep so that when she awoke, she could complete her work.

CHAPTER ELEVEN: THE GIFT

THE SIXTH DAY OF CHRISTMAS

*W*illiam leaned over his anvil, sweat dripping off his chin as he panted from the exertion of his work. It was early. Too early for any of his men to have arrived at the smithy, but he had not been able to sleep, so eventually he had given up and left his bed.

The lock was almost complete.

If only he knew what was happening with his sunshine. He had been keeping his distance, not trusting himself to be near her. His desire to be with her was overpowering, but he had to give her time.

William had been both elated and apprehensive to observe the ducal carriage arriving on Market Street. The duchess had kept her word about visiting Caroline. But had he made the right decision to intervene between the two childhood friends?

And if it healed her soul, but he lost her forever because

of his autocratic meddling, would it be worthwhile to know she had reclaimed her self-respect?

Raising a hand, he combed it through his damp hair and thought about the possibility that they might never be man and wife. Could he live with it if she was happier now? If he had helped her find the respite she needed, even if she would not forgive him for what he had done?

Since his night with Caroline, his nightmares had not returned. Now his dreams were haunted by something much worse. When he fell asleep, he would dream of her. Like sunshine breaking through the clouds of winter, his joy had no bounds to be reunited with her once more. To touch her. Talk with her. Experience the pleasure of her company.

But, inevitably, he would awaken to find himself alone in the dark.

Caroline had shown him how to live again, and he did not desire a return to his solitary existence since returning from war. He wanted to live. To feel. To experience life with her. To witness her generosity of spirit when they brought their future children into the world.

To him, she was the very embodiment of the holiday season, and he wanted her by his side every day from here on forward for the rest of his life. He wished he could walk out of the smithy and just go find her. Talk to her right now. But he was determined to allow her an opportunity to lay her past to rest and heal. His impatience to seek her out did not signify.

What had happened during the duchess's visit? Had Caroline found the peace she so desperately needed? Or did she hate him for his bungling interference?

* * *

HER GRACE WAS NOT COMING.

Caroline had been waiting for her arrival all day. Long shadows out on the street revealed it was now late afternoon. It was clear the ducal carriage was not returning as the duchess had promised.

Caroline traced a finger over the delicate embroidery. She had pulled the floss out and redone it several times. Absolute perfection was needed, and she had worked the coat of arms until her fingers ached with exhaustion.

It was all for naught.

She sighed heavily.

Was it a sign? While she had worked on the gown, she had swung back and forth over whether she should seek William out. The duchess's decision not to return for the gown proved Caroline had not earned her forgiveness in any genuine sense. She could only be grateful that the noblewoman had seen fit to visit her at all.

"Mrs. Brown, would you like me to make you some tea?"

Annie's expression displayed concern. The girl had been hovering, clearly worried at her employer's demeanor. Though Caroline had attempted to maintain a cheerful countenance, her disappointment must be apparent.

"That would be lovely, Annie."

Caroline smoothed out the gown, gently folding it in silver paper and wondering what she would do with it. Her own desire to wear it had vanished because, in her mind, it already belonged to Her Grace. Perhaps she would have it delivered to Avonmead so she could finish this matter and begin a new chapter.

Attempting to take stock of her emotions, Caroline pondered what came next.

Packing the folded dress into a box, she carried it to the back and placed it on a shelf before joining Annie at the fireplace for tea.

Just as she picked up the cup and saucer, she heard the

front door open and close. Setting her cup down, she hurried to the front to find that Her Grace had finally arrived. Caroline's spirits ascended so sharply she felt dizzy.

"Mrs. Brown! I apologize for our delay. We had some trouble with one of the carriage wheels, and the duke wanted to ensure it was repaired while there was still daylight. Their endeavors appear to be successful, but we will have to fly home come first light to make it to Avonmead for our Old Year's Day celebrations."

The ducal carriage could be seen through the window, and the duke and the coachman were standing behind it and discussing something about one of the large rear wheels which they were inspecting.

"I thought you had changed your mind, Your Grace."

The duchess shook her head. "Never! My word is my bond."

"I am so happy you are here."

"As am I. Is the dress complete?"

Caroline's chest tightened in nervous anticipation. She had been so careful with the sewing of the Halmesbury emblem, knowing it had to be exact. "I shall collect it from the back."

Caroline hurried to collect it from the shelf, pausing while she admitted that butterflies had taken flight in the region of her stomach. So many hours had been poured into making the gown over the past few months. Every spare minute she had found had been invested into it, but the final work had been completed overnight and throughout this morning. Was it the same high standard as her prior work?

It is my best work, so it will have to do.

Lifting the box, she carried it to the front, placing it on the counter. Her Grace came over, and Caroline opened the box to lift the gown out. Carefully unfolding it, and pushing the silver paper to the side, she presented the gown.

The duchess gasped, both hands fluttering up to cup her cheeks in amazement. "Oh! It is beautiful. You are an artist, Caroline!"

Caroline inhaled roughly, not realizing she had been holding her breath until air rushed back into her lungs. "Truly?"

"It is breathtaking. Heraldic. May I try it on?"

"Of course."

She led the duchess to the back.

Annie stood at the fireplace, her jaw hanging open and her eyes wide at the fine noblewoman accompanying her employer before collecting herself to drop into a curtsy. "Milady."

Caroline realized Annie had not been present when the duchess had visited the day before. "May I present Miss Annie Greer, Your Grace?"

"Your Grace?" The girl's eyes had widened even more, if such a thing were possible. "Cor!"

The duchess grinned. "It is my pleasure to meet you, Miss Greer. How do you enjoy working for Mrs. Brown?"

"I love working here … Your Grace."

"She is a remarkable artist. You will learn much as her apprentice."

Annie nodded effusively in vigorous agreement.

Caroline assisted the duchess to divest her carriage dress and then to don the walking dress before standing back to admire her work. Her Grace's chestnut hair was vibrant in contrast to the Prussian blue velvet. And from the back, the coat of arms in golden floss was as striking as she had imagined.

Viewing the gown in the mirror from different angles, the duchess returned to the front to show it to the duke, who had entered while they were in the back. His gray eyes lit with appreciation as he smiled fondly down at his wife.

"Is it not splendid, duke?"

"It is, but it cannot rival the beauty of the wearer."

The duchess laughed sweetly, blushing in pleasure while brushing her hand over the front of the gown and fiddling with the buttons. "I adore it, Mrs. Brown. It is truly unique. I shall wear it when we visit our tenants on New Year's Day. I think it will create quite a stir at Avonmead."

Caroline exhaled heavily as the past vanished and her unencumbered future arrived. "I am so pleased to do this for you."

Once she packed the dress back into its silver paper and box, the noble couple took their leave. Caroline walked out behind them to watch their departure in the gray light of twilight, waving to the duchess as the carriage pulled forward.

Looking down, she realized Annie had come out to stand beside her.

"Will I make a gown for a duchess one day, do you think?"

"Anything is possible if you work hard and practice."

"The dress was very beautiful, Mrs. Brown."

"Thank you."

"Are you sad it is not to be yours like you intended?"

"Not at all. I did not realize it at the time, but it was always destined to belong to Her Grace. Everything is as it should be."

Caroline accepted the truth of it.

Two years ago, she had not the means to repair what she had done. In the interim, she had worked hard to further her skills, even when there had been no hope of owning her own shop. When the opportunity had presented itself to pursue her dream, in the form of Lord Saunton's apology and offer of amends, she had seized it to make her dream come to fruition. Then, as a final step, she had expressed her gratitude to Miss Annabel and completed the dress. The garment had been a method of proving herself, but sacrificing it to regain her self-respect felt right. Its value had grown by gifting it to the person who deserved to have it.

Of course, her happy ending had been facilitated by a certain blacksmith who had seen fit to meddle.

What was she to do about William?

* * *

WILLIAM WAS STANDING on the road outside the smithy, taking a break from the heat of the forges to enjoy the wintry chill, when he spotted the ducal carriage driving along Market Street.

The duchess had returned for a second visit? He supposed that must be a promising sign that the past had been laid to rest.

He still had trouble remembering that he had had the audacity to demand an audience with the wife of a duke. Not just any duke, but the Duke of Halmesbury, one of the most revered peers in the realm.

Should he attempt to visit Caroline to see where he stood with the modiste?

Peering down at his disheveled attire, which was soaked in sweat from toiling since before dawn, and his soiled hands covered in soot, he thought not. Considering the lateness of the hour, perhaps he should not attempt to visit her today.

In the morning.

He would visit her in the morning so he could look his best. Perhaps, if things with the duchess had gone well, they could court. He wanted that outcome so much he could taste it.

* * *

CAROLINE PACED BACK and forth in her rooms as she considered and reconsidered showing up unannounced. The landlady had retired to her rooms three hours earlier and was sure to be asleep by now. Changing her mind a hundred times, she was too agitated to rest while trying to decide.

In the distance, she could hear the clock chiming midnight in the sitting room. Biting on her fingernail, she once again debated visiting William. The streets should be deserted, and William was only a few blocks away. If she visited him, she could find out where matters stood between them.

Making up her mind, Caroline donned her cloak and raised the hood in case she encountered anyone in the street.

Quietly, she exited the cottage, hurrying down the street to turn in to the alleyway which would lead to the end of Market Street. To William. She could have waited until morning, but then she would have to see him at the smithy, where they could not speak freely.

It was still Christmastide. The holiday magic was not over. Perhaps they could reach an understanding.

Approaching Mrs. Heeley's cottage, she was reassured to see it enshrouded in darkness. Passing by, she reached the blacksmith's back door and prayed the lock would still be broken. If William was in bed, and the door had been repaired, she would have no method to gain his attention and would have to return home, unsuccessful.

Which would mean that all she would have achieved this evening was making herself very bloody cold for no reason.

Extending a hand, trembling with icy stiffness, she reached for the door handle.

* * *

WILLIAM LAY AWAKE, staring at the ceiling. Considering his plan to visit Caroline in the morning, a bit of sleep would not go amiss. Nevertheless, he had lain awake for the past hour, wishing he could see her tonight. Some instinct kept urging him to resolve this matter with her. It seemed imperative that they hold on to the magic of the festive season or risk losing each other forever.

It was all very melodramatic; he had told himself many times. Yet, still, he could not shake the notion that their destinies were entwined and he should not waste this reprieve from loneliness.

His gloom was interrupted when he heard the creak of his stairs. Sitting up in alarm, he listened closely. It sounded like someone was climbing them!

He made to rise, but then the humming started, causing him to blink and lie back. Apparently, he had fallen asleep without realizing it and was dreaming of her once more. Was it to be like the dreams from Christmas Eve? A visitation in which she revealed some truth to him?

> *Should auld acquaintance be forgot,*
> *and never brought to mind?*
> *Should auld acquaintance be forgot,*
> *and auld lang syne?*

The door of the bedroom next to his creaked as it was opened and then shut, and the humming grew louder, approaching the door of his bedchamber.

> *And there's a hand, my trusty fiere!*
> *and gie's a hand o' thine!*
> *And we'll tak' a right gude-willie waught,*
> *for auld lang syne.*

He frowned, uncertain of his conclusion. If this were a mere conjuring in his dream, Caroline would sing the English lyrics he was familiar with, not the original Scottish lyrics which he did not know?

Through the gloom of night, he could just make out the door swinging open in the moonlight. There she stood, sunshine draped in that silly green cloak she loved so much.

"Caroline?"

"You should repair your back door. Since it is gone midnight, I suppose I can wish you a happy Old Year's Day, blacksmith."

"Is it you? Are you truly here?"

She made a low sound, humming a bar of the song that marked the end of the year. "I was thinking about what you did for me. I thought you might like to know what happened … or perhaps you might want to speak with me."

"I do."

She exhaled deeply, apparently needing to hear this. His sunshine might exude confidence, but it was apparent she had been uncertain of her welcome.

"Why are you here?"

"It did not seem fair that you gave me such a wonderful gift, but I have given you nothing in return. So I came to bring you one. If you want it."

"A gift?"

"It is tradition to give gifts during Christmastide."

"What is it?"

"Me. If you still want me?"

His heart leapt, drumming into high speed in his chest. With that, she crossed the room, coming to stand by the edge of his bed. She unbuttoned her cloak to shrug out of it and let it fall at her feet, revealing that she was dressed only in a night rail. Kicking off her shoes, her hand reached for his counterpane to pull it back.

"Wait!" It was incomprehensible that he had stopped her from joining him in his bed, but he had to know. "Is this a temporary gift?"

He waited with bated breath for her answer. If she were only here for the night, he must deny her. He could not go through it again. Losing her several days earlier had been hellish.

Nothing had brought any lasting solace, not even work as it had done before.

He had worked late into the night, coming home to fall into an exhausted heap on his bed, yet still he had found no respite from the aching loss of her presence. He had seen the future—what it could be—and it was too agonizing to have it ripped away a second time.

"I have to leave before dawn."

His heart stopped, and he abruptly changed his mind—he wanted to grab this time, cherish it like a man condemned to die come morning. He could not possibly deny himself a few stolen hours of joy before returning to the black misery he had been experiencing without Caroline to light the shadows.

His dreams were vastly improved, but his waking hours had become pure hell. Knowing she was just down the street. Fighting the urge to run to her and sweep her into his arms, ignoring any protestations about the terrible mistakes of her past.

"But once the banns are read, I think we can make this a permanent arrangement."

He gasped out loud as his hopes came thrumming back to life.

"You … are accepting my proposal?"

"Make space, blacksmith. I wish to lie in your arms."

Oh hell, his eyes were moist. He whipped the counterpane to the side and then reached out to grab and pull, causing Caroline to fall over him with a giggle. She felt soft. And cold. That ridiculous cloak needed to be replaced.

"You are exquisite and wonderful and exasperating … and come tomorrow, I will visit you so you can explain what happened, but now …"

"Now?"

"Now you will pay." With that, he gave a playful nip to her chilled shoulder, causing her to yelp and squirm against him, her mound grinding against his groin in the most appealing manner. Their mouths fused together in hungry abandon as desire mounted. Their hands feverishly exploring to divest nightclothes until passion overcame them and found its way to its inevitable conclusion. Finally, they lay panting on their backs in the spent aftermath of their lusty entanglement.

William grabbed hold of his discarded nightshirt to clean her and then himself, before tossing it in a ball on the floor. Then he drew her into his arms, tucking her close and leaning forward to kiss the crown of her head. "I shall have the vicar read the banns on Sunday."

She huffed and wiggled her naked buttocks more firmly into his lap, re-igniting the fire in his loins. "Can you not afford a Common License so we do not have to wait three Sundays, merchant blacksmith?"

Warm pleasure sang through his veins at the question, veritable sunshine stealing through an overcast sky to light his soul from within. She was in a hurry to wed him!

"Termagant!" She giggled, wiggling closer. "I suppose that can be arranged, but I shall have to make a display of courting you come morning if we are to wed that soon."

"Tomorrow, or rather later today, I shall close my shop early for Old Year's Day if you wish to spend some time with me in the afternoon."

"Aye, we will make a show of it for our neighbors."

"And you can accompany me to church services on New Year's Day."

"Aye, I shall arrange with the curate to share a pew with you at services."

"It is settled then, blacksmith."

"Aye, modiste."

"William … I did not tell you how I raised the loan for my shop."

He heard the hesitation in her voice, and realized she must have a little more to confess. But tonight was for savoring their new future together, and the details of how she had arrived in his life did not signify. That was the past and this was their present.

"It will not alter my feelings. Let us enjoy the holidays, and we can settle all our matters once the banns are read."

She was quiet for several moments, presumably thinking on what he had said. Finally, she responded, "You are a good man, William."

Caroline went quiet after that. Hugging her close, William listened to her breathing as she slowly fell asleep in his arms, his broad grin of sheer happiness fixed in place. He could scarcely comprehend how much his life had changed in a matter of days. Solitude and darkness were in the past. Sunshine would light his way as he walked into his future.

Every day, from this day on, would be Christmas with Caroline at his side.

EPILOGUE: THE NEWS

JULY 1821

My dearest Mrs. Jackson,

Mr. Thompson and I are returning to Chatternwell to meet with the earl's Master Builder and highly anticipate meeting your esteemed husband. Would you consider joining us for dinner after Sunday service on 22 July? If you are agreeable, we could send our carriage to collect you and Mr. Jackson to bring you to Chatternwell House. I do hope you can join us!

Warmest regards,

Jane Thompson

Caroline was humming in the sitting room when William came downstairs. He could live a hundred years and never grow weary of hearing his sunshine's melodies. With a smile, he entered the room to find Caroline sitting at the table with a cup of tea. It was evident she had already eaten before he had descended. Their new housekeeper, who was cleaning up, greeted him as she walked past to leave the room. "Good morning, Mr. Jackson."

"Mrs. Marlowe." He nodded. Walking over to the place set for him, ducking slightly to avoid the beams of the ceiling, William gave Caroline a quick kiss before taking his seat. Mrs. Marlowe returned with a plate of eggs and ham to set before him.

"Thank you."

The housekeeper nodded in acknowledgment and left them alone.

"Annie came by this morning to inform me that Mrs. Greer has accepted an offer of marriage from Mr. Andrews."

"At last! Mrs. Greer is a good woman and certainly deserves an improvement in her circumstances."

"I am very pleased. Once she weds, Mrs. Greer will probably be helping the baker in his shop, so perhaps I shall find another widow for the work she has been doing for us. It has been rewarding to help a member of our community with enterprise."

William nodded. "That would be excellent. What of Annie?"

"I informed her that if she were to want to apprentice with the baker instead, I would be agreeable with releasing her from our contract, but she said she enjoys making pretty things."

"That was kind of you to offer." William reached out to caress her soft hand.

Caroline nodded. "I thought it was important to verify that her interests had not shifted. She has learned much over the months, so I was relieved she wished to continue on with me."

"I am gratified to hear that, considering the upcoming changes to our lives. I am looking forward to meeting Mr.

and Mrs. Thompson after services today. He is an excellent architect from all accounts, so we should have an interesting conversation. Perhaps he can apprise me of the latest developments in London."

His wife tucked an errant lock of flaxen hair behind her ear, her eyes shining in the morning light. "And I cannot wait to hear the latest from Town. Mrs. Thompson is well-versed in fashion, it being a special interest for her."

"Will you inform her of our news?"

Caroline tilted her head thoughtfully before glancing down at her belly. "Not yet. Even your uncle and aunt do not know yet. We shall visit them so they can be the first to know. They are the only family we have, after all."

William rubbed a hand over his beard, thinking about how they would react. Would it be the good news that brought hope back into their lives, as he had dreamed so many months earlier? They certainly had responded warmly to his letter that he had married. "Thank you for thinking of them."

"Of course."

"You look lovely."

Caroline glanced down again. She was wearing her mulberry dress, one of his favorites. "The fichu is delightful, is it not?"

William squinted at the lacy gauze that shielded her bosom. "Not as delightful as what it concea—"

She groaned, dropping her forehead into her hand in agony. "Please do not finish that sentence! I am so happy I can discuss fashion with someone who truly appreciates it later today!"

He chuckled, lifting her smaller hand in his to plant a kiss on her smooth knuckles. "I am and always will be a blacksmith, my love."

"That is more than apparent." Her tone was scolding, but

her hazel eyes were warm with affection as she smiled back at him.

* * *

WILLIAM AND BARCLAY—THE architect had insisted conversation would be much easier if they dropped the formalities—were in a spirited discussion regarding the lock that William had recently perfected.

"Do you mind if we leave the table, my dear?"

Jane Thompson smiled at her husband, shaking her head. "The meal is mostly over. Please go ahead."

William threw a glance at Caroline, clearly seeking her assent. She gave a nod, and the two men sprang up to leave. Barclay Thompson, a tall man with a fall of black hair and a beard similar to her own husband's, wanted to collect the lock from the smithy. He had expressed an interest in part-nering with William to have the lock produced in London using his contacts. Barclay foresaw great potential for profits if they were to form a venture together.

"I have to admit I could no longer listen to the merits of brass versus zinc in the internal mechanisms of a lock," Jane professed once they had left the room.

"Can I go read my book?" Little Tatiana looked up from her plate to address her stepmother, her deep blue irises riveting and her silver-blonde hair escaping her plait. The little girl would be a true beauty in a few years.

"Of course. Mrs. Jackson and I will be here if you need anything."

The little girl grinned, obviously bored by the chatter of adults. Rising quickly, she scampered from the room in a flurry of skirts, leaving Caroline and Jane to enjoy picking at the vestiges of their meal.

"I wanted to comment on your fichu. The lace is very delicate."

Caroline fingered the lace edge carefully. "It was a wedding gift sent to me by the Duchess of Halmesbury."

"Oh! You know the duchess? The duke is Barclay's cousin!"

She nodded. "I was in service for the Baron of Filminster at Baydon Hall as a girl. When Her Grace was merely Miss Annabel."

Jane was biting her lip, an expression of worry marring her features. "I do not suppose news has reached Chatternwell yet."

"News?"

Her hostess appeared nervous. "I am not sure I should inform you, but you will hear of it soon and you might want to send Her Grace a letter."

Caroline grew alarmed, a nervous flutter beginning in her belly. Whatever Jane was thinking of was clearly a distress. "What is it? Has something happened to Her Grace?"

Jane shook her head. "Not directly …" She nibbled her lip, evidently trying to decide what to say. "We nearly postponed our trip here because there is something of a family emergency in London. The earl insisted that we were not specifically needed and should continue with our plans."

"What is it?"

Jane swallowed hard, clearly reluctant to impart what she knew. "I regret to inform you that the baron was murdered three nights ago in his London townhouse."

"What?" Caroline clapped a hand over her mouth, realizing she had shrieked.

"I am … sorry."

"I barely spoke to the baron, but how is Lady Halmesbury?"

"She is taking it in her stride, but she is very upset at the allegations that her brother is the perpetrator of the crime. I wanted to remain in Town, but Lady Saunton is assisting her and insisted she and the earl would see to Her Grace's needs."

"Master Brendan! That is not possible. He is the most amiable of men! And what was the baron doing in London? He never travels out of Filminster."

"He was in Town for the King's coronation. I do not know what the outcome of the allegations against her brother is because we left on Friday for Wiltshire. Lord Saunton and the duke were in communication with the coroner. We are cutting our trip short a few days to return as quickly as possible. I am so sorry to be the one to inform you of such terrible tidings."

Caroline waved a hand. "Thank you, Jane. I would prefer to hear from you rather than the news sheets. I shall write a letter of condolence this evening."

"Her Grace will appreciate it, I am sure. I do not get the sense she was particularly close to the baron, but her concern for her brother is grave. If he is arrested and found guilty, he could hang …" Jane shook her head so that her ebony locks bounced in the light.

"This is ridiculous. Why would he do such a thing? They have the wrong man!"

"I agree. Mr. Ridley is one of the warmest gentlemen I have met. You should see him with Jasper."

"Jasper?"

"His nephew—the duke's heir. Mr. Ridley has a wonderful way with children. He would not commit such a heinous act of violence. This is an elaborate misunderstanding based on coincidences. It is my hope the actual perpetrator will be discovered by the time we reach London."

"I hope so, too. It is distressing to think of Her Grace being caught up in this situation. She deserves better."

"I agree. If you wish to write her a letter, I can provide

you with access to the library and take it back with me to deliver by hand? We are returning on Tuesday, so she will have it before the week is out."

Caroline nodded. "That would be lovely."

* * *

LATER THAT NIGHT, Caroline slipped into bed next to William. Cuddling up to him, she put a slim arm around his waist to stare pensively at the opposite wall.

"Do not be distressed, sunshine. The duchess has many connections to assist her in the matter, and the duke is very influential. If anyone can sort out this muddle, it will be him."

She smiled tremulously. William pushed his concern for Caroline to the side, leaning down to kiss her temple. "Her Grace is surrounded by many allies. You can only control what you do here in Chatternwell. You should find someone to take over the work of Mrs. Greer. Someone who works hard and deserves our support."

Caroline nodded, leaning her head back to gaze at him in the darkened room. "You are a good man, William Jackson."

"And you taught me to count my blessings, Caroline Jackson. You are my greatest blessing of all."

"Until our babe comes along."

He chuckled, embracing her close. "Until our babe is here. Then I will have all the riches in the world."

"Are you and Barclay to do business together?"

"I think so. He was impressed with the design. With the type of connections he has, we are sure to find the right men to work with."

"I am glad. Perhaps with his help, you can spend more time on creating designs."

"As long as I live here with you for the rest of my days, anything I do for income is a blessing."

She smiled, her cheek pressed against him as she slowly drifted off in his arms. "I love you, blacksmith."

"And I you, sunshine." William held her close, thankful to the universe for the sunshine in his life which would multiply further with the arrival of their first babe. Caroline's current distress for the duchess made him ache, but the fact that he was able to comfort and support her in her time of need was a blessing to be cherished. They were a family now, just as he had dreamed of all those months ago.

UNRAVEL THE MYSTERY of the baron's death, and discover if a marriage born of scandal can become a true love match in *Long Live the Baron*.

AFTERWORD

When I first wrote down the idea for this book, I had no idea how much research I was setting myself up for. Although plenty is known about the peerage, diving into trades and working classes presented all sorts of challenges, extending past the limits of my previous knowledge of the Regency.

Thankfully, a weekend in Colonial Williamsburg fleshed out a lot of information about both American and British trades and how day-to-day business was conducted during the period.

Thinking I was back on track, I was thrown another curve ball when my "easy" research for the holiday season turned out to be in conflict, so I had to dive deeper than expected to straighten out the discrepancies and uncover the truth.

But what fun it has been to research dress-rooms, black-smiths, and Christmas!

Holiday traditions in the period differed from region to region, but the ones I mentioned are among those practiced in the Regency era.

There is conflicting information about the exact dates of

the Christmastide calendar, but I am reasonably confident I got it right using Chambers' 1869 printing of *The Book of Days*, along with the celebrations calendar for the Church of England and a variety of other sources, including Charles Dickens himself.

The lyrics of *Twelve Days of Christmas* are a version taken from an anonymous broadside published in Newcastle between 1784 and 1825.

The lyrics to *Auld Lang Syne* are Robert Burns's version from 1788.

To my knowledge, it did not snow on December 24, 1820 in the Bath district, but it may have. I could not locate any details of the weather that day, so I did not write in conflict with any known weather from the day.

During the Regency, one generally rented a space in a pew or had to stand in church, which is why William needed to visit the curate on Old Year's Day—now known as New Year's Eve—to arrange to share a pew with Caroline.

The silver paper used by Caroline to pack the walking dress was similar to white tissue paper, but brighter, more translucent, and stronger than what we are familiar with today.

Curious about the treatments Dr. Hadley prescribed for William's sprain and his deep concern regarding the injury? William Buchan wrote about strains in his 1790 book, *Domestic Medicine*:

> *Strains are often attended with worse consequences than broken bones. The reason is obvious; they are generally neglected. When a bone is broken, the patient is obliged to keep the member easy, because he cannot make use of it; but when a joint is only strained, the person, finding he can still make a shift to move it, is sorry to lose his time for so trifling an ailment. In this way he deceives*

*himself, and converts into an incurable malady what might have
been removed by only keeping the part easy for a few days.*

The skirmish at Hougoumont Farm is based on accounts of the day, and Corporal Graham was selected by the Duke of Wellington as the bravest non-commissioned officer at the battle of Waterloo.

When I set out to write *The Duke Wins a Bride*, it was without the knowledge that the next several books would turn into a series redemption arc, bringing us back full circle to The Stable Incident, but that is how it played out. The incident which started it all turned out to have a butterfly effect as each story idea unfolded in my mind.

Now that we have finally returned to the duchess, a new arc begins with her brother and the unresolved issues he has with the man everyone believes to be his father.

Lord Josiah Ridley, the Baron of Filminster, returns to wreak havoc on Brendan's state of mind before inconveniently being murdered. Brendan will need all the support he can get when an ambitious coroner plans to issue a warrant for his arrest. Even the powerful Duke of Halmesbury might not stop this tide of injustice.

It might require an Inconvenient Bride to step into the breach and save Brendan from the Tower of London. An ingenious young woman who has been developing her intellect by reading books since her cousin recommended a certain text on military strategy.

All will be revealed in *Long Live the Baron*.

ABOUT THE AUTHOR

Nina started writing her own stories in elementary school but got distracted when she finished school and moved on to non-profit work with recovering drug addicts. There she worked with people from every walk of life from privileged neighborhoods to the shanty towns of urban and rural South Africa.

One day she met a real life romantic hero. She instantly married her fellow bibliophile and moved to the USA where she enjoyed a career as a sales coaching executive at an Inc 500 company. She lives with her husband on the Florida Gulf Coast.

Nina believes in kindness and the indomitable power of the human spirit. She is fascinated by the amazing, funny people she has met across the world who dared to change their lives. She likes to tell mischievous tales of life-changing decisions and character transformations while drinking excellent coffee and avoiding cookies.

ALSO BY NINA JARRETT

INCONVENIENT BRIDES

Book 1: The Duke Wins a Bride

Book 2: To Redeem an Earl

Book 3: My Fair Bluestocking

Book 4: Sleepless in Saunton

Book 5: Caroline Saves the Blacksmith

INCONVENIENT SCANDALS

The Duke and Duchess of Halmesbury will return, along with the Balfour family, in an all-new suspense romance series.

Book 1: Long Live the Baron

Book 2: Moonlight Encounter

Book 3: Lord Trafford's Folly

Book 4: Confessions of an Arrogant Lord

Book 5: The Replacement Heir

* * *

BOOK 1: THE DUKE WINS A BRIDE

Her betrothed cheated on her. The duke offers to save her. Can a marriage of convenience turn into true love?

In this spicy historical romance, a sheltered baron's daughter and a celebrated duke agree on a marriage of convenience, but he has a secret that may ruin it all.

She is desperate to escape...

When Miss Annabel Ridley learns her betrothed has been unfaithful, she knows she must cancel the wedding. The problem is no one else seems to agree with her, least of all her father. With her wedding day approaching, she must find a way to escape her doomed marriage. She seeks out the Duke of Halmesbury to request he intercede with her rakish betrothed to break it off before the wedding day.

He is ready to try again...

Widower Philip Markham has decided it is time to search for a new wife. He hopes to find a bold bride to avoid the mistakes of his past. Fate seems to be favoring him when he finds a captivating young woman in his study begging for his help to disengage from a despised figure from his past. He astonishes her with a proposal of his own—a marriage of convenience to suit them both. If she accepts, he resolves to never reveal the truth of his past lest it ruin their chances of possibly finding love.

Can be read as a standalone book or as part of the Inconvenient Brides series of Regency romance books.

* * *

BOOK 2: TO REDEEM AN EARL

A cynical debutante and a scandalous earl find themselves entangled in an undeniable attraction. Will they open their hearts to love or will his past destroy their future together?

She has vowed she will never marry...

Miss Sophia Hayward knows all about men and their immoral behavior. She has watched her father and older brother behave like reckless fools her entire life. All she wants is to avoid marriage to a lord until she reaches her majority because she has plans which do not include a husband. Until she meets the one peer who will not take a hint.

He must have her...

Lord Richard Balfour has engaged in many disgraceful activities with the women of his past. He had no regrets until he encounters a cheeky debutante who makes him want to be a better man. Only problem is, he has a lot of bad behavior to make amends for if he is ever going to persuade Sophia to take him seriously. Will he learn to be a better man before his mistakes catch up with him and ruin their chance at true love?

Can be read as a standalone book or as part of the Inconvenient Brides series of Regency romance books.

* * *

MY FAIR BLUESTOCKING: BOOK 3

A young woman who cares little about high society or its fashions. A spoilt lord who cares too much. Will they give in to their unexpected attraction to reveal a deep and enduring passion?

She thinks he is arrogant and vain …

The Davis family has ascended to the gentry due to their unusual connection to the Earl of Saunton. Now the earl wants Emma Davis and her sister to come to London for the Season. Emma relishes refusing, but her sister is excited to meet eligible gentlemen. Now she can't tell the earl's arrogant brother to go to hell when he shows up with the invitation. She will cooperate for her beloved sibling, but she is not allowing the handsome Perry to sway her mind … or her heart.

He thinks she is disheveled, but intriguing …

Peregrine Balfour cannot believe the errands his brother is making him do. Fetching a country mouse. Preparing her for polite society. Dancing lessons. He should be stealing into the beds of welcoming widows, not delivering finishing lessons to an unstylish shrew. Pity he can't help noticing the ravishing young woman that is being revealed by his tuition until the only schooling he wants to deliver is in the language of love.

Will these two conflicting personalities find a way to reconcile their unexpected attraction before Perry makes a grave mistake?

Can be read as a standalone book or as part of the Inconvenient Brides series of Regency romance books.

* * *

BOOK 4: SLEEPLESS IN SAUNTON

An insomniac debutante and a widowed architect befriend each other. Will little Tatiana finally get the new mother she longs for before this country house party ends?

In this steamy historical romance, a sleepless young woman yearns for love while a successful widower pines for his beloved wife. Hot summer nights at a lavish country house might be the perfect environment for new love to bloom.

She cannot sleep ...

Jane Davis went to London with her sister for a Season full of hope and excitement. Now her sister is married and Jane wanders the halls alone in the middle of the night. Disappointed with the gentlemen she has met, she misses her family and is desperate for a full night's sleep. Until she meets a sweet young girl who asks if Jane will be her new mother.

He misses his wife ...

It has been two years since Barclay Thompson's beloved wife passed away. Now the Earl of Saunton has claimed him as a brother and, for the sake of his young daughter, Barclay has acknowledged their relationship. But loneliness keeps him up at night until he encounters a young woman who might make his dead heart beat again. Honor demands he walk away rather than ruin the young lady's reputation. Associating with a by-blow like him will bar her from good society, no matter how badly his little girl wants him to make a match.

Can these three lonely souls take a chance on love and reconnect with the world together?

Can be read as a standalone book or as part of the Inconvenient Brides series of Regency romance books.

* * *

BOOK 5: CAROLINE SAVES THE BLACKSMITH

A fallen woman. A tortured blacksmith. When the holidays force them together, can they mend their broken hearts?

She has a dark past that she must keep a secret. He has a dark past he wishes to forget. The magic of the festive season might be the key to unlocking a fiery new passion.

She will not repeat her past mistakes ...

Caroline Brown once made an unforgivable mistake with a handsome earl, betraying a beloved friend in the process. Now she is rebuilding her life as the new owner of a dressmaker's shop in the busy town of Chatternwell. She is determined to guard her heart from all men, including the darkly handsome blacksmith, until the local doctor requests her help on the night before Christmas.

He can't stop thinking about her ...

William Jackson has avoided relationships since his battle wounds healed, but the new proprietress on his street is increasingly in his thoughts, which is why he is avoiding her at all costs. But an unexpected injury while his mother is away lays him up on Christmas Eve and now the chit is mothering him in the most irritating and delightful manner.

Can the magic of the holiday season help two broken souls overcome their dark pasts to form a blissful union?

Can be read as a standalone book or as part of the Inconvenient Brides series of Regency romance books.

* * *

BOOK 6: LONG LIVE THE BARON

A new baron accused of murder. A young lady who knows he is innocent. When she helps free him, they will be forced to marry. Can their mutual dislike lead to true love?

A steamy historical suspense romance, about a young woman driven to do the right thing, a lord who does not quite appreciate the gesture, and a murder investigation that could end their new relationship before it begins.

Her conscience drives her to act ...

Miss Lily Abbott knows the new baron is innocent because she saw him entering the widow's home next door at the time of the crime. But when the widow refuses to assist him, this young woman who hoped to marry for love cannot stand idly by when she knows the truth. Lily risks everything to provide an alibi for the glib gentleman who barely remembers her name.

He can't believe he has to marry her ...

Lord Brendan Ridley stands accused of patricide to gain the title he now holds. Not even his close family connection to the powerful Duke of Halmesbury can help him. He prays his paramour will come forward to clear his name, but honor dictates he not reveal his whereabouts that night without her consent. When help comes from an unexpected quarter, he finds himself forced to marry an annoying chatterbox to save her from scandal.

When these two mismatched people are forced to marry, will they find a way to work together to reveal an enduring passion before the real murderer strikes again?

Can be read as a standalone book or as part of the Inconvenient Brides series of Regency romance books.

Printed by Amazon Italia Logistica S.r.l.
Torrazza Piemonte (TO), Italy

54204703R00109